Stories by Stephen Carey Fox

The End of Illusion
The German, 'Mr. Kai' and the Devil
Artists, Thieves & Liars
Of Margaritas, Piña Coladas & Mint Juleps
The Collector
Lou & Billy Joe
The Ghost of Yesterdays
Blame Jason Bourne
A Most Improbable Union
Everybody Knew ... Nobody Knew
Awakening
'When the Bough Breaks'
The Best Laid Plans
The Robin Hood Solution

The Elephant in the Room

'A Well-regulated Militia'

Stephen Carey Fox

The Elephant in the Room

'A Well-regulated Militia'

This is a work of fiction. Unless otherwise indicated, all the names, characters, businesses, places, events and incidents in this book are either the product of the author's imagination or used in a fictitious manner. Any resemblance to actual persons, living or dead, or actual events is purely coincidental.

ISBN: 979-8821757081

www.mickeysgod.info

Are all the laws, but one, to go unexecuted, and the government itself go to pieces, lest that one be violated?

Abraham Lincoln (1861)

♠

There is danger that, if the court does not temper its doctrinaire logic with a little practical wisdom, it will convert the constitutional Bill of Rights into a suicide pact.

Robert H. Jackson's dissent in
Terminiello v. Chicago (1949)

♠

'When you find the Colonel, infiltrate his team by whatever means available and terminate the Colonel's command.'

'Terminate the Colonel?'

'Terminate with extreme prejudice.'

Apocalypse Now (1979)

♠

ONE

He was gone. In his sleep. It took everyone by surprise. As full of life at sixty-three as one could imagine of someone that age. Some remembered that Franklin Roosevelt, who was not healthy, had died at the same age under circumstances that initiated unfounded conspiratorial speculation.

Once the days of shock and mourning had passed and conspiratorial speculation set in, the death of Justice Angus Wilson left President Gloria Addison with plenty to think about.

An associate justice of the United States Supreme Court, Angus Wilson had led the court's influential originalist clique. Some believed tradition demanded the president's nomination to replace him should refill the empty originalist slot on the Court. The president would then face the distinct possibility that Wilson's replacement would not share her judicial philosophy.

But the president wasn't the only actor in this drama. Both political parties had to approve her nominee. Could she find a person with a reputation for independence who could satisfy the requirements of both? Someone in the middle? She was certain someone so bland did not exist.

♠

Wilson's unexpected passing convinced President Addison to take another difficult decision. She should, she believed, suggest to Ms. Wilson—for reasons not entirely honest—that an autopsy would provide her relief by explaining her husband's death. Beyond that the president wanted to scotch any notion of foul play. The latter, that slight bit of dishonesty, she would not mention to the widow. The distraught Ms. Wilson—Phyllis—and 'The Chief' agreed to the autopsy.

The result allowed the president and presumably Ms. Wilson to breathe a little easier: Angus Wilson had a defective heart. Dr. Richard Glass told Phyllis and Chief Justice Clarence Smallwood, that her husband and his revered associate died from a congenital defect, *hypertrophic cardiomyopathy* (HCM). No one in sixty years had detected it in Angus Wilson.

"You mean to tell me when he went to camp as a kid?" Phyllis Wilson asked with common sense logic.

"When he played high school football? When he joined the Marines? Not even when the president nominated him for the Court? No one? Ever?"

"Ms. Wilson, allow me to offer you my condolences for your loss. Your husband's service to the country was exemplary and much admired."

"Thank you, doctor."

"Now, as to your question about previous diagnoses, I'm afraid the answer is, yes, it was most definitely possible for his condition to go undetected."

"How could that be, doctor."

"Ma'am, HCM is not unknown, but it's rare, which fits your husband's situation. The reported prevalence of HCM ranges from 1 in 200 to 1 in 500 people in the general population. But we think as many as 85 percent of those who have it go undiagnosed."

"Did he inherit it?"

"It's possible. HCM can run in families, But not all cases of HCM are genetic. I'd have to review his family's medical history before I could even begin to answer your question, Phyllis."

"What makes HCM so dangerous?"

"The heart muscle pumps oxygen-rich blood around the body by contracting and relaxing. With HCM, the walls of the heart become thicker than normal. This can cause the heart to become more stiff, leaving less room for blood to fill the heart ...

"A heart affected by HCM must work harder and may have difficulty pumping oxygen-rich blood to the rest of the body. As a result, those with HCM can experience a lack of energy, a fast heartbeat, chest pain, or other symptoms."

"That explains a lot that I noticed about him lately. Thank you, doctor."

"Excuse me, Ma'am," Dr. Glass replied, "what did you notice? It would help me provide a more solid post-mortem diagnosis if you could be specific."

"Well," she looked down, thinking, "not so much the chest pains but a lack of energy and rapid heartbeat. I know that because we have one of those small blood pressure monitors. The kind you wrap around your wrist."

"I see. I'll add that to my notes. What was his pressure—on average?"

"High. 212/110. That's too high from what I've read or heard on TV."

"I'll say! Was that consistent? I mean, consistent lately?"

"I'm not sure. He didn't share. I only saw the one reading over his shoulder."

♠

Angus Wilson's passing and the choice of his replacement rekindled concern in some quarters about the honesty of the men and women in courtroom black who swore not to put their hands on the scales of justice. Perhaps the sincerity behind this critical oath depended on what was meant by 'hands' and to whom such hands belonged.

Wilson had been on the Court for twelve years, the titular leader of its originalists, or textualists. He and his fellow intellectual travelers belonged to The Federalist Society for Law and Public Policy Studies or, more plainly,

The Federalist Society. Wilson had once been the society's president.

One vote short of a Court majority, the Society's successful nominees, including Angus Wilson, piously vowed that *they* would interpret the Constitution as intended by those who drafted and voted to ratify it. They would not be putting *their* hands on the scales of justice; in reality, they had the temerity to insist, those hands would be those of the Founders.

Their message, then, was unmistakable: only they possessed the insight necessary to read the Founders' minds. Doubtless, that was a great and useful thing to believe and to claim—persuasive also to a gullible public—that only *you* understood what everyone else saw as an enigma. Those not smitten by the originalist argument saw only bravado—chutzpah—and an agenda run amok.

♠

Thus, the death of Justice Angus Wilson, as with all unfilled Supreme Court vacancies, unleashed the furies. Each side in the debate viewed control of the court as political control of the country, the ultimate thwarting of their enemies' evil designs.

A man, or woman, wields great power when alive. But dead? Sadly, quickly forgotten. Poor Angus Wilson. He was barely in the ground when speculation began about his replacement. A fear arose in the party opposite, fed by its hyperbolic media cohorts, that the president and her congressional allies intended to use the opportunity, if it one can call someone's death an 'opportunity,' to pass a bill creating additional judges—to pack the court with justices aligned philosophically with the president. Why so?

Each time President Addison's party lost the White House, a frequent outcome, the opposition had managed, fortuitously in some instances, or through the application of raw political power at other times with no slight amount of hypocrisy, to replace retiring or deceased justices with partisan justices of their choosing.

Consequently, every program put forward by Addison's party faced an ignominious death at the hands of the Supreme Court. What to do? One possibility? Do exactly as the opposition forecast. Add justices sympathetic to the current administration's agenda. Pack the court before you lose the next election. Angus Wilson's death was not the first occasion that such a scheme had crossed the mind of President Addison and others in her party. There was precedent.

Addison's thinking differed little from President Franklin Roosevelt's proposal to increase the number of justices to regain political control of the Court to protect his pet political projects (not stated out loud, of course). It should not have escaped the Addison administration's attention that Roosevelt's plan backfired dramatically.

The opposition knew of such a strategy, of course, and it served only to embolden them further, and they plotted accordingly. The president would have to walk on a fine line, thread the needle, so to speak, to achieve a satisfactory outcome. She would need to find a compromise candidate, one, as mentioned, that both sides could accept as an acceptable substitute for the originalist Angus Wilson.

♠

TWO

President Gloria Addison removed her outer mourning clothes and tossed them carelessly onto one of the facing divans in the center of the Oval Office. She had just come from Justice Wilson's burial at Arlington National Cemetery. Her chief of staff, Sean McKinnon, an Irish Catholic transplant from Boston to Columbus, Indiana, pulled up a chair next to Addison's desk, famously known as the *Resolute* desk.

"Stephanie!" she spoke sharply but not unpleasantly to her executive assistant over the office intercom even before she took her seat behind the enormous Oval Office desk. "Get me the AG."

'Stephanie' was Stephanie (not her Vietnamese name) Quach of Ho Chi Minh City who the president had known since their days at Cummins. She was a small woman, as Vietnamese always appeared to be in the presence of Americans, and quite beautiful. At formal White House parties, she always wore her homeland's traditional *áo dài*, which invariably created a bit of a sensation and led to a trail of wannabe suitors following close behind. Whether the tongues of Stephanie's courtiers hung out … Well, that's best left to the imagination.

Stephanie's family had fled Vietnam in the late 1970s as part of a group collectively known as the 'boat people.' Stephanie never spoke of it, and no one dared ask, how many of her relatives had died in the 'American War,' as the Vietnamese called it, fighting for the South or with the Viet Cong.

What remained of the Quach family made it into that small craft and eventually settled in Columbus. Stephanie got a job at Cummins after completing her education, and she became friends with and an admirer of Gloria Addison. The respect was mutual.

After calling the attorney general's office, Stephanie announced that Vice President Xavier Ortega was standing next to her desk.

"Good," she replied as Ortega, who had decided not to wait for an invitation to enter the Oval, came through the curved door at the side of the room. His initiative did not sit well with the president.

"Have a seat, Xavi," she said in an expressionless voice that belied her pretense at congeniality. "We're waiting for the AG to call back."

♠

Xavier, or Xavi, or Javi Ortega was both an odd and an obvious choice for Gloria Addison's running mate. Unlike her personal history—no serious impediments to her rise in politics—Xavi's was a classic rags-to-riches story.

Xavier Ortega's story began in the southernmost Mexican state of Chiapas before he was born. Adverse economic and political conditions there persuaded the Ortegas and thousands of others to undertake the long and arduous journey north. Jorge, Esperanza and their two small children crossed into New Mexico near El Paso. Did they have papers? Of course not. But they had what American employers of cheap, agricultural workers wanted: strength of purpose, strong backs and hope. Xavier Manuel Ortega was born near Albuquerque six months after his family's arrival.

Later, when he became an athletic and political celebrity, publicity about Xavier Ortega boasted that the pugilist-turned-politician had begun to work the fields with his family before the age of five. Whatever the truth of that claim, which Xavier always laughed off, he knew what the fields and landowners took from his parents with insufficient return. He vowed that working the fields would not make an old man of him, as it had his father by his fortieth birthday.

In his late teens, young Xavi took his strong back, muscled arms and abandoned the picking fields of Albuquerque for what he envisioned as a place to use that strength and talent in the fight world of the cities of the southwest. As he trained and occasionally fought, he took evening classes at UNM, the University of New Mexico in Albuquerque and eventually earned a college degree. In the ring, he became the middleweight champion of his state whose renown spread beyond. These were not accomplishments that many could pull off; they did not go unnoticed.

Those who knew how to advantage themselves of the popularity of men like Xavier Ortega eventually pulled him from the sporting limelight into the political. At first, Xavi was having none of it, and he held out for a surprisingly long time to such blandishments—but not forever. Egos are just that, egos.

From afar, Gloria, a closet boxing enthusiast, had heard of a former boxing phenom now climbing the political ladder in New Mexico. Critics, she read, described him as charismatic, cut from the mold of a Muhammed Ali. She wanted to know more. She watched his career blossom. She listened to his speeches. One couldn't say definitively when it happened, but eventually Gloria joined the ranks of those who strove to break through what she believed was only a veneer of resistance and offer him useful purpose in service to hers.

"He can help us," she insisted to Sean.

The decisive moment for both parties came when the nominee had to pick a running mate. In hindsight, there was never a possibility she would overlook Xavi Ortega, and she didn't disappoint. They met. They spoke. And she picked him over the traditional list of aging white men handed her and a much smaller number of promising women. Passing over the latter pained her, but she believed she had to do it. Finally, no small part of her decision to offer Ortega the vice presidency was the advantage it would give her, she assumed, with Hispanic voters.

Gloria's offer managed to break Xavi's resistance to those who could advance him. Gloria's overture was, he rationalized, a 'useful' opportunity.

♠

The president looked around the room as she tapped her fingers on her desk. After a few seconds of silence, she spoke.

"Sean, you know the story behind this desk?"

"Can't say that I do, Madam President."

"You, Xavi?"

"I'm as clueless as Sean, I'm afraid."

"Well, we've got some time. Simon is not a prompt man, so, listen up, and, like I said, don't worry about the AG. He never returns my calls on time. Still pissed about the nomination fight, I expect. So, we have some time to kill, unless either of you have something really pressing for me."

"No, Ma'am. Nothing that can't wait."

"No, Madam president," Ortega echoed.

It was obvious to McKinnon that the president *wanted* to tell them the story of the desk.

Stephanie, with a knowing smile on her face, left her desk to close the Oval door. She'd overheard the story a half-dozen times.

"Anyway," the president began, "they built this desk from the oak timbers of the British Arctic exploration ship HMS *Resolute*. Queen Victoria presented the colossal object in front of to President Hayes in 1880 as a gift. It's also called the 'Hayes desk.'"

"There's more. Interested?"

"Sure," Ortega replied with disguised prevarication. He decided silence was the best strategy.

"Years earlier, in 1854," the president pressed on, "the captain of *Resolute* abandoned the ship in the Arctic waterway while searching for Sir John Franklin and his lost expedition ...

"The Franklin expedition met with disaster after becoming icebound for more than a year. Franklin and nearly two dozen others died after they abandoned their ships. The survivors set out for the Canadian mainland and promptly disappeared ...

"The Admiralty launched a search for the missing expedition in 1848 and searches continued for decades. Eventually, they recovered several relics from the expedition, including the remains of two men returned to Britain. A series of recent scientific studies performed on the remains suggested the expedition's men did not die quickly. Hypothermia, starvation, lead poisoning, or zinc deficiency and disease presumably killed everyone. Cut marks on some of the recovered bones suggested postmortem consumption of their fellows—possibly cannibalism ...

"The crew of *George Stephanie*, an American whaler, found the *Resolute*, repaired it and returned it to Britain as a gesture of goodwill."

"Come to think of it, Madam President," Sean piped up. I think I had heard some of those details before, or perhaps I read them in *The Smithsonian* or *National Geographic*."

Vice President Ortega stayed out of it.

"Probably," the president concluded, not hiding her irritation with his remark. She was certain he already knew the story and had let her run on.

♠

The *Resolute* desk. President Addison had considered storing it. Its unflattering size dwarfed her 115-pound, 5'2" frame. Not exactly the fit a Commander in Chief needed to make others in the Oval feel small, which in the case of Gloria Addison was essential to the point of obsession. Command yes, pretense no, ruthless perhaps. None of those, however, with those dimensions. And she'd seen all three practiced in that office.

Take those photos of LBJ's 6'4" frame, weight unknown but 260–280 would be a good guess, towering from the advantage of a desk chair pulled up close to a subject in need of the president's cajoling, intimidating someone sunk deeply into the cushions of one of those low divans, deliberately made soft, one suspects, for such occasions. Now that was command, pretense and a kind of ruthlessness. But Gloria Addison wasn't 6'4" and 270 pounds. Maybe storing the *Resolute* was a public relations fight she didn't need. Stephanie and Addison's chief of staff, Sean McKinnon, had advised against removing the best of *Resolute's* remains from the Oval.

A few moments later Stephanie announced the return call from the attorney general.

♠

THREE

"The AG on one, Ma'am."

"Thank you, Stephanie," she said sweetly. "General?"

She pronounced it 'Gen-ur-ul,' all syrupy and southern Indiana-like.

"Yes, Madam President. That was quick! I just got back to the office myself." A lie. "What can I do for you?"

"Simon, you know damn well what you can do for me! So, let's cut the pleasantries and get on with it. I need you here at the White House, pronto! You gonna have any problem with that?"

"No, Madam President. May I ask the agenda?"

The Supreme Court, Simon! A replacement for Wilson. That enough of an agenda for you?"

"I'll be there as soon as I can. How's thirty minutes?"

"Fine, fine, thanks."

♠

There was a reason she sounded short with him; at least in her mind there was a reason. Attorney General Simon Jordan, an African American and descendant of slaves, whose necessity for glasses gave him a bookish appearance, hailed originally from Aliceville, Alabama. As a boy, he had arrived in Buffalo, New York, via one of the later versions of the original Underground Railroad 'freedom trains.' Simon's grandfather had chosen that path quite unintentionally when the Jordan family finally had enough of the Jim Crow South.

No less ambitious politically than the vice president and armed with having survived, integrity intact, and occasionally had his way in the notoriously cutthroat political world in Albany, he had tried to wrest the party's nomination from Gloria Addison two years earlier. His appointment as attorney general took most of Washington's pundits by surprise.

For Gloria Addison, however, adding her rival to the cabinet was mostly the point. She figured he could never threaten her if he were in the administration, and she would have him where she could keep an eye on him, make sure he wasn't plotting a coup or something. She also knew him to be a capable lawyer and administrator.

Attorney General Jordan arrived forty minutes later. The president wasted no time in coming to the point. She didn't mind putting him on the spot whenever the opportunity to do so arose.

"Who you got lined up to replace Angus, Simon?"

"Let me look. Just a moment."

She thought there was a good chance he didn't have any lists, and what she was about to hear would just be BS. The expression on her face suggested that to McKinnon, who threw his head back in mock laughter.

He had an answer quicker than she expected.

"Ten on a long list and three on the short one," Jordan replied.

"Well, we need one that's out of the box, someone unpredicted but not unpredictable. I'm also thinking about the *bigger* picture. And I mean that literally. You get my drift?"

"You want to expand the court."

"Damn! Speaking of predictable. You know the trouble with you, Simon, is you can always read my mind ... up to a point."

"How many, Madam President?"

"What's realistic?"

"Well, you're up against a 6-3 lineup now, with you on the short end. You'll always need an odd number to break ties, so, adding four gets you to 7-6 to the good—ideally. That'd take the court to thirteen alright, but a 7-6 margin is still too close for comfort. So, I believe you're lookin' at six for minimal comfort. Gives you a 9–6 advantage with a little room to spare for the possibility of deviant behavior."

"You mean the ingrate asshole or the ingrate assholes."

"Right."

"Well, FDR couldn't get it done. What're our chances? Tell me how it might work."

"The Constitution says nothing about the number of justices, only that there shall be a supreme court and inferior courts ..."

"It calls 'em that? 'Inferior Courts'?"

"Yes, Ma'am. Created by Congress."

"Jeez ..."

"In their defense, they meant 'inferior' differently. Courts at a lower level, not inferior in an intellectual sense."

"Yeah, yeah, I get all that!"

"But there is an opening that justifies more justices. It comes from Alexander Hamilton ... *Federalist 78*. Congress pays their salaries. Congress 'commands the purse' ... et cetera, et cetera ..."

"Get to the point, Simon, please."

"So, Hamilton opined that because Congress pays their salaries, Capitol Hill has all the license it needs to control the number of judges. And, from time to time, Congress and state legislatures have done so ... but always for the political advantage of one side or the other."

"Which brings us to the current Congress."

"Right. The Constitution isn't the problem, Madam President. It's Congress. You don't have the sixty votes you'll need in the Senate to end cloture."

"Okay, I need to have a 'Come to Jesus' talk with our majority leader. Any chance he'll get the Senate to axe the filibuster to help me out?"

"Slim to none, Madam President. Everyone will see your—his—purpose is political, and they won't go for that. I doubt he could even get fifty-one votes, either to end the filibuster or to do anything to the Court other than replacing Angus."

Ortega now felt it was time for him to go on record.

"I agree, Ma'am. The Senate and the American people would view that move as a politicization of the Court and unacceptable."

"So, the minority leader and his party get to act politically whenever they want, but our majority can't. That's not what they teach you in political science or government classes. What kind of BS *is* that?"

"Minority rule, Madam President. That's how the Senate operates, which, unfortunately, is consistent with the un-democratic construct of that body … and the Constitution, for that matter."

"Simon, you keep telling me stuff I know. I hired you to tell me stuff I *don't* know."

Her irritation at his condescending tone showed.

"Yes, Ma'am. I'm Sorry."

"Okay, Simon," she sighed. "Send over your long and short lists."

"You want me to talk to the majority leader?"

"No, I'm not going that way. We've just got to pick the most suitable, the most reliable person. Someone we can count on every now and then. Any women on your *long* list?"

Jordan looked up then back at his list. He knew what was coming.

"Two."

Gloria knew he had the lists with him, because twenty percent seemed about the right allocation for a government dominated by men.

"Out of ten?"

"Yeah."

"Jesus H. Christ! Did you not hear me say just two minutes ago 'someone out of the box'? And the *short* list?"

"What do you think?"

"Goddammit, Simon, stop sounding like a patronizing sonofabitch. I want to *hear* you say it!"

"Are you recording this?"

She stood, glaring at him.

"Are you trying to get yourself fired? Did you not hear what I just said? You ought to know better than to pull that Nixon s**t on me. Are there any women on your short list, Simon? That's a simple question. Say it!"

"None."

"No shit! Well, that's a real shocker, Mr. Attorney General," a conclusion that no one in the room could mistake for anything other than sarcasm.

She was about to throw caution to the wind which wasn't the first time when it came to Simon Jordan.

"We'll see about your 'none!'" she barked. "Maybe I'll replace *you* with a woman!"

She wouldn't, of course, and he knew it. She needed his political instincts and influence for the battle ahead.

♠

FOUR

Two hours after her frustrating discussion with the attorney general on how best to proceed with a nomination to the Supreme Court, President Addison met again with Jordan, Ortega and, additionally, Oregon's senior senator, Philip Clark, the majority leader. McKinnon sat in.

"I'm going to weigh right in on this, folks, so fasten your seatbelts. Phil, Simon's got a long and a short list of qualified candidates. He says there're two women on the ten-person long list, and not one on the short list of three …

"So, here's what's changing. We are moving the two women on Simon's long list to the short one and dropping two men, and don't any of you give me that crap about no women being qualified!"

"Jesus, Gloria," the vice president whined, "this is pretty short notice ..."

McKinnon took his nose out of the briefing book in his lap. Addison glared at her vice president.

"Xavier, it's 'Madam President,' and Jesus has nothing to do with what's happening here ...

"Phil, I want you to look at Simon's lists and tell me who on those lists is confirmable. I'm going to assume the two women are confirmable. That's the bottom line here, gents. Pick your top guy from the three currently on the short list to go with the women. Chuck the leftovers. That leaves three. Got it?"

The three men nodded obsequiously.

"We'll reconvene in fifteen minutes."

♠

Thirty minutes later.

"Okay, Xavier, what've we got?"

"Madam President, the three of us are recommending that we sit on this for a few days. Our advice to you is that a move like this requires more time. We think the country deserves that."

"All of you agree?"

The three men nodded.

"Well, here's another way of looking at it," President Addison replied. "My way. We're going to decide right now and tell the country later. No one will be the wiser. Look, besides picking a judge I've got a country to run. I'm obliged to move things along on a priority basis. So, tell me. Who's on the short list?"

"Madam President, Phil Clark replied, we've done what you asked about the women, but we expanded the short list to four."

"You added a third woman?"

All three squirmed in their chairs and cleared their throats as one.

"No Madam President," Clark spoke for the three, "we think you ought to consider this fellow Cavendish from Rhode Island."

"You tellin' me, Phil, that someone I never heard of is better than all the highly-qualified women in this country?"

"No, Ma'am," the vice president leaped into the breach, "but honestly, he's more qualified and confirmable than most women. More experienced behind the bench ..."

"More experienced comin' from a piss-ant state like Rhode Island? What can that be worth?"

McKinnon gave her a look that suggested caution.

"It's just a political reality, Madam President. I think you'd find his views on church and state interesting. Eventually, the court will get around to deciding the Montana case on public prayer. Everyone opines it will be landmark. Cavendish could be a useful ally."

"You lecturing me on political reality and who might be a 'useful ally,' Simon? Seems like we settled that at the convention."

Another look of caution from McKinnon.

"No, Madam President. The reality is that Phil says he can't get a woman confirmed. Any woman."

She glared at the majority leader.

"Have you tried, Phil? You got *any* votes?"

She didn't give him time to answer.

"Obviously, you haven't tried. You just assume you can't do it, or you're too goddam lazy!"

McKinnon cleared his throat.

"May I speak candidly, Madam President?"

"I assume you always do, Phil," she said in a tone that no one present understood to be anything but sarcastic. Phil Clark chose to ignore the slight.

"I know the Senate, Ma'am. I've breathed Senate air for the past 32 years. I know it like nothing else. Respectfully, I'm the majority leader by the will of the voters of my state and my colleagues. No one else. On the other hand, Xavi and Simon are on you. Nothing that happens here this afternoon is going to change that. Respectfully."

"Respectfully, Mr. Majority Leader, what place does the country occupy on your list of those to whom you believe you must answer? Yes, you are the senior senator from Oregon, and you have an obligation to listen to your constituents. However, if I recall my political science correctly, you also have a duty to follow your conscience, to act at times as you think best *for the country*! You are also a free agent."

"Respectfully, Madam President, this may not be one of those times."

His cavalier answer stunned her. The majority leader of the Senate had just abandoned his responsibility to lead … *to her face*! He, in fact, *had* no ability to lead, she realized. Jordan and Ortega knew it, too.

She looked at the trio knowing she had lost. She gave them as hard a time as she could, and they didn't cave. Yes, they didn't cave, but all three stood for weakness, not strength.

"Okay," she relented with a sigh, "who's the fourth candidate ... Oh, yeah, you mentioned this Rhode Island guy named Cavendish … By the way, let's cut to the chase. How's he on the Second? That's why we've been having this conversation."

The three men looked at each other, helplessly, then back to the president.

"When I looked at his résumé, I didn't see anything that could guide our thinking about him," Jordan said.

"That makes no sense to me," Addison replied. Who in hell doesn't have an opinion on the Second? Especially judges? So, he's a stealth something or other. S**t! …

"You know what I'm thinking about this right now?" she asked.

They hadn't a clue how to answer that question. But before any of them could make up something to say, the president answered herself.

"Most of those seven words George Carlin says you can't repeat on TV! Now, unless you want to hear those words from the mouth of a woman, all three of you get the hell out of my office and get to work on this Judge Cavendish. I don't want any surprises."

The President of the United States may have studied political science, but she hadn't grasped, or chose not to grasp, the Founders' reasoning behind and insistence on a separation of powers. She was the president, responsible for executing the government. No one else had that power, and she intended to wield it for what she thought fit.

"Sean, over the next few days I want you to go up to Capitol Hill and start getting a sense from our senators how they might feel about a change in their leadership."

McKinnon looked at the woman across the desk, weighing carefully what he should say next. He thought he saw not a president but just someone he had seen at Cummins. That vision shook him, and he decided on a kind of intervention.

"Frankly, Ma'am, they might tell me that a change in leadership ought to start right here, in the Oval Office."

"You get the hell out of here, too, Sean!"

♠

FIVE

Gloria Addison's political career had begun suddenly, precariously, and, in the end, successfully. Unmarried at forty-one, her ambition was unfulfilled in her position in the personnel department at Cummins in Columbus, Indiana, an energy company heavily invested in diesel engines, natural gas engines, and alternative fuel engines. She'd been at Cummins for fifteen years and five before that as one in a stable of secretaries at a law firm.

Gloria had majored in business and psychology at Indiana University. She was a good student, graduating with an average located generally in the 3.0 to 3.5 grade range. But her curiosity and promise, according to her faculty advisor in the business department, exceeded those statistical markers.

At Cummins, she had helped to solve collective and individual problems: she took the lead in salary negotiations, securing health insurance, retirement planning, and the preparation of Wills. But those essential tasks convinced her she was a wasted talent, that she could do even more for more people.

Her parents and teachers had instilled in Gloria a belief in the value of public service as a duty of citizenship, an expression of patriotism. Harold and Bernice Addison talked incessantly to Gloria and her two brothers, Tom and Bill, about the meaning of the war and necessity for sacrifice on the home front as well as the war front. They waxed rhapsodic about the country's willingness to rally behind the powerful contrasts the president drew between enemy ideologies and actions, and American democratic ideals, purposes, and determination.

Gloria Addison's patriotism was not maudlin, sugary, or sentimental ... but it was aggressive and subject to her interpretation. She believed the brand of American patriotism preached by her parents had faded almost entirely, and she wanted to do something, however small, to remind the country of its greatness and possibilities, which, of course, did not make her unique. What was unique was her determination to do something about it. But where to start?

She decided to run against the county commissioner representing Perry Township. That would install her as one of the five commissioners who constituted an executive board to make decisions for the entirety of Bartholomew County. True, the county needed fresh blood and fresh ideas, but Gloria's ambition, which had an edge on the dark side—cut-throat if you must know—far outpaced the need to fix potholes, answer constituents' complaints, and shake up the commissioners' ranks.

♠

A testing engineer named Sean McKinnon also worked for Cummins. McKinnon had a BS from Purdue University and a GPA slightly higher than Gloria's. McKinnon also chafed at Cummins. A kind of stagnation. When he learned she was thinking of entering politics, he suggested she ought to hire him as campaign manager on a voluntary basis. He'd seen her potential. Seen how she was with people. A natural politician. Small but feisty. Some rough edges, sure, but McKinnon was a huckster. He'd smooth some of those edges and hide what he couldn't. Unmarried like Gloria, what was there to lose?

Gloria loved the huckster quality in Sean. Peas in a pod. They belonged to the same poker club. She'd seen the bravado, the ability to bluff the socks off lesser players, the payoff.

She won that first campaign, which was not without controversy about her undeserved and unnecessary personal attacks on her opponent, a man named Clinton Downey who sold insurance—or tried to—in Columbus.

With that victory something special entered her bloodstream: politics and winning. She brushed off the complaints about her use of character assassination. Politics and winning had the same effect on Sean.

No sooner had she gone to work for the county when, pushed along by McKinnon at moments of waning confidence, she began to eye other political horizons.

In short order she won a seat in the state assembly, employing again the tactics that got her that seat on the board of commissioners where she pushed for commonsense programs aimed at helping the middle class, possibly as penance. Accomplishment there and a growing reputation for legislative victories led to a successful bid for the state senate.

She called for a complete overhaul of the state's income and property tax structures. She wanted to end the traditional tax code by which working-class families subsidized millionaires who often paid tax at the same rate as a family of four or no tax at all. As for property taxes, she sought to guarantee people did not lose their homes due to increased assessments when homeowners had made no improvements. Senator Addison also found it necessary to ask probing questions about recycled subjects—farm subsidies, bad roads, and the status of schools and education—traditionally avoided by more cautious politicians or those who had discovered ways to benefit financially (graft) from doing nothing or resorting to meaningless platitudes designed to obfuscate or confuse.

Sean McKinnon kept alive his reputation as a master obfuscator and bamboozler as well as campaign manager. He succeeded in keeping the interest of the media and public in his candidate through humor and guile.

A frequent 'complaint' from Gloria about his performances went something like, 'Jeez, Sean, did you really say that?' Or 'Jeez, Sean, how am I ever going to live up to your bullshit?' Invariably, his answer was a smile and a new quip or piece of legerdemain at the next press conference. The man was incorrigible.

Then, Gloria Addison grasped the opportunity to go national. She had challenged the sitting senator from Indiana, Alva Richards, for the nomination to run for the U.S. Senate and lost. Her first. But Richards, 93, now running for his ninth term—ninth!—keeled over at one of those infamous chicken-salad fundraising lunches and died. He should have had a food tester. Other diners, all younger in varying numbers, got by with campylobacter or something uncomfortable but less threatening. Poor Alva. How was he to know he was just too old and his former rival too ambitious.

The admired and feared state senator from Columbus insisted she be handed the now empty nomination. Her logic was hard to resist. She had finished closest to Richards in the primary; no one else was close. According to the party's rules, the nomination belonged to Gloria Addison. She leaped to grasp it!

Alva had hardly turned cold when there was a United States Senator Gloria Addison—by a wide margin. But it was all too easy and bound to get tougher the higher she climbed. She didn't think much of the tough part, though, being so fixed on the climb and the prize. Sean McKinnon, who should have been whispering cautions in her ear, wasn't.

She waited a year, did little or nothing of note in the Senate, then, egged on by McKinnon, although she needed little outside encouragement, launched a presidential bid on a snowy day in Columbus.

Gloria's pitch to voters was not how she would fix a laundry list of issues, although she had answers, workable or not, for all of them. Apparently, voters didn't need her solutions to make up their minds. Gloria Addison was a breath of fresh air. She'd play to her strengths: affability and energy. Seeing her on the debate stage, fidgeting, throwing up her arms when she wanted to make a point, tossing her head around as though it were on a swivel, mocking the competition—to see all that side by side with the familiar bevy of middle-aged white men … well, size didn't matter. Her *joie de vivre* and dismantling of those men was more than sufficient to send voters to the polls in astonishing numbers.

By all accounts her ascendancy to the presidency had been a tour de force. She had won the nomination over Simon Jordan and six others and bested her opponent in November by eleven points. But that wasn't good enough for President-elect Addison. Johnson had defeated Barry Goldwater by twenty-two!

When she mentioned that statistic to ger best friend back home, the friend's reply, like so much else about Gloria's political run, should have been sobering. The friend reminded her that Johnson, once the maestro of the Senate and later the surprising inspiration for a civil rights agenda on Capitol Hill that he choreographed from the White House, refused to run again when challenged by two senators and antiwar mobs in the streets, effectively resigning the presidency years ahead of his successor's more ignominious leaving two years after he crushed George McGovern by twenty-three points.

"If you are going to measure yourself against Johnson and his twenty-two points, to say nothing of McGovern," Barb Sanders warned the president-elect, "those are comparison you should reconsider. Be careful, honey. Just remember where you come from. If you do that, you'll be fine."

It was advice that would have profited President Addison to heed.

♠

SIX

Judge Randolph Cavendish. No one thought the position suited him or that he was suited to it. No one in the legal profession. No one in the Republican Party hierarchy. No one in the Senate, except for the majority leader whose concern was practicality, he told the president, not suitability.

What the critics meant by 'suitability' wasn't what others might have thought. Those who thought him ill-suited meant they didn't understand him, could not appreciate his attachment to where he came from and the values of that place, his background, his lack of ostentatiousness. That was why they didn't trust him. They couldn't understand him. Didn't *want* to know him. Perhaps that did qualify him as unsuitable. But the president wasn't buying.

'Practicality' or 'suitability.' He was the practical choice, therefore a suitable choice. A matter of semantics, perhaps. But the choice of a replacement mattered to the President of the United States, and she wasn't interested in parsing words.

Gloria Addison shared the majority leader's reverence for practicality, but in the end, hers was the only opinion that counted. She needed ... wanted to trust him, to count on him. She heard what she wanted to hear. Not from the vice president; not from the attorney general. The majority leader assured her she could bank on Randolph Cavendish, the practical choice, to sanctify her agenda with a Constitutional blessing.

♠

Enter Randolph James Cavendish, bachelor and scion of an old, very old, New England family, not Mayflower old, but of voyagers thereafter out of Sudbury, Suffolk County, England. The towns and cities near Sudbury carried familiar names: Ipswich, Felixstowe, Clacton-on-Sea, a bit further Chelmsford in Essex County, Norwich of Norfolk County to the north, Cambridge a few miles west, and London itself southwest.

Five centuries later focus had shifted to a Cavendish out of Cranston, Rhode Island, our Cavendish, an unabashed devotee of the state's colonial founder, Roger Williams (more on that in a moment), and an associate justice of the United States Court of Appeals for the First Circuit.

Randolph Cavendish began life in Mattapoisett, Massachusetts, the third child—Elizabeth and Eunice preceding him—of Henry James Cavendish and Catherine Ann Bell. Henry Cavendish moved his family to Cranston, a suburb of Providence, due, presumably to enhance his law practice under the umbrella of the two largest cities in the state. Cranston, the Chamber of Commerce boasted, had a vibrant suburban community with abundant rural areas and a shoreline on beautiful Narragansett Bay. Randolph, or 'Randy,' his mother's affectionate way of addressing him, had just turned 9 at the time of the move.

Young Cavendish cobbled together an enviable academic record. Valedictorian of his high-school class; matriculation to Harvard University and a *summa cum laude* degree in history and induction into Phi Beta Kappa. He concluded his formal education with a bachelor's degree from Harvard Law School.

If one could say it of anyone, one might say of Randolph Cavendish that it's possible to be born wealthy, positioned for a life of privilege with any whim fulfilled, and just sit back and let the ride take you along. Of course, it's also possible to attain a position of limitless advantage through one's own efforts. Which described Randolph Cavendish?

He eschewed every modern convenience other than a refrigerator and a television—black and white, of course. He loved the natural world and became a driving force behind PETA (People for the Ethical Treatment of Animals), and he spent as much time as his responsibilities away allowed mountain climbing in New England. He had 'conquered' New Hampshire's Mt. Washington,

Vermont's Mt. Mansfield, and Maine's Mts. Katahdin and Sugarloaf numerous times.

Reportedly, a client once asked, "Why go back again and again?"

"Oh," he replied thoughtfully. "It's different each time and each season."

♠

Another interest of Cavendish was history. It should not surprise that it wasn't modern history that fascinated the judge. Rather, his taste ran to 17th century religious history, early statements about the separation of church and state, and thus to perhaps the most famous Rhode Islander, Roger Williams.

Roger Williams was born in or near London probably in 1603. His father, James Williams, was a merchant tailor, and his mother, Alice Pemberton, one can assume, a housewife.

Williams received a respectable education: Charterhouse School and Pembroke College, Cambridge. At the latter he became a Puritan and thus ruined his chance for preferment in the Anglican church. In 1629, he married Mary Bernard, the daughter of a notable Puritan preacher and author. Mary and Roger would have six children, all born in America.

Williams knew that Puritan leaders planned to migrate to the New World. He did not join the first wave of settlers but later decided he could not remain in England under the administration of the Anglican Archbishop. Williams regarded the Church of England as irredeemably corrupt and false.

"One must separate from it to establish a new church for the true and pure worship of God."

Having become a separatist convert, Roger and Mary sailed for Boston in late 1630.

Williams moved from Boston (Salem to be precise) to Plymouth Colony in 1631 where he regularly preached. William Bradford, the colony's governor, said 'his teachings were well approved.' Soon, Williams found the Plymouth church insufficiently separated. His contact with the Narragansetts also caused him to question the validity of colonial charters that did not include legitimate purchase of Native American land. He even charged that King James had uttered a 'solemn lie' in claiming he was the first Christian monarch to have discovered the land. Governor Bradford became disillusioned with Williams's positions, and he and Mary returned to Salem.

In late 1633 the Massachusetts Bay authorities summoned him to appear before the General Court in Boston to defend his tract attacking the King and the charter. The parties managed to smooth out the issue. But in early spring 1635 the General Court ordered him to appear. There was no smoothing out this time. His 'erroneous' and 'dangerous opinions' resulted in his removal from his church position.

Exasperated with Williams, the General Court tried and convicted him of sedition and heresy in fall 1635 and ordered him banished. He traveled 55 miles through deep snow, from Salem to Raynham where local Native Americans supported him until spring, when Williams and others from Salem began a new settlement in Rumford, Rhode Island on land which he had bought from Massasoit.

Eventually, Williams established a new, permanent settlement. Under the belief that divine providence had brought them there, the settlers named the settlement 'Providence.' Williams had founded the first place in modern history where the state and religion were separate, combined with the principle of majoritarian democracy.

Regarding the issue of church and state, Roger Williams declared the state should concern itself only with matters of civil order.

"It must confine itself to those Commandments of the ten that pertain to relations between people."

He described the attempt of the state to pass laws concerning an individual's religious beliefs as a 'rape of the soul' and spoke of the 'oceans of blood' shed from governments' attempts throughout history to command conformity. None of those governments had the authority to promote or repress any religious views, he believed. Most of his contemporaries disagreed.

Neither mountain climbing nor eccentric clerics interested those in charge of Cavendish's vetting. After days spent with the judge, intensive questioning of those who knew him best, and painstaking, thorough analysis of his writing, the president's emissaries reported back that he seemed perfectly suited to his job if not its trappings. It wasn't a full-throated endorsement for a position on the Supreme Court, but filling a seat there was always a crapshoot.

The investigators also learned that Cavendish wasted little time establishing a career after Harvard Law. After laboring for two years as an associate in a private law firm, Randolph realized he disliked private practice and accepted a position as an assistant attorney general of Rhode Island. There, he gained prosecutorial experience. In short order the attorney general selected Cavendish to be the Deputy Attorney General. Eventually, he succeeded the outgoing attorney general.

Apparently, Cavendish wasn't so enamored of the prosecutorial role in the law as he first thought. He moved quickly to the bench, first as an associate justice of the Rhode Island Superior Court, then as an associate justice of the state Supreme Court. By the time of his vetting

Cavendish had seven years of judicial experience at the appellate level, four years at the trial court level, and ten years with the attorney general's office. While serving on the Court of Appeals he took his place on Simon Jordan's long list to fill Angus Wilson's seat and then, due to the machinations of the president, found himself on the short list.

SEVEN

"Good morning Madam President."

"And to you, Sean. What've you got for me this fine morning?

"Nothing pressing."

"Oh, darn!" she said sarcastically, smiling.

"Recent polling looks good."

"Oh yeah? Which one?"

She paid attention to only one. The chief of staff's reference to 'polling' was a tongue-in-cheek word game they played whenever the polls came out.

"Gallup. National approval. You're just under fifty."

"Over fifty anywhere?"

"Vermont."

"Jeez, Sean. How many voters live there?"

"Not enough."

They both laughed.

"Heard anything from the home front these days?"

She didn't expect he had any news from Columbus, but she wanted to make small talk and could think of nothing else.

"Funny you should ask today. There's one thing that got my attention. They're having a 'remembrance' tomorrow for Freddy Agabashian."

"Huh? Oh, yeah. My Dad told me some stuff about him. Did the 500, right?"

"Fifty-two, Ma'am."

"Just once?"

"I believe so."

"Way before my time! But I do know he drove our car. What happened?"

"He qualified on the pole; set a track record. After that, not so well. Apparently, the car overheated during the race. Picked up rubber on the track. Clogged the turbocharger's cooling system."

"Shame."

"Fred is in the National Midget Auto Racing Hall of Fame … and the Indy Hall of fame."

"I think we should send something, don't you?"

"Yes. It's an important day for the company and Freddy's family."

She picked up the phone and pressed the button for her assistant.

"Stephanie, please call the florist when I'm through with Sean. On his way out he'll give you the info you need."

♠

"Ma'am?" Sean McKinnon returned to White House business. His face suggested a seriousness absent during the Agabashian discussion.

"Yep?"

"The top item this morning is Judge Cavendish."

She gave him a look of frustration.

"I asked before what you had for me! Why'd you wait until now to tell me this?"

"The Senate is set to grill him next week. There is also speculation the Court will hear oral arguments on the Columbia, Missouri, assault weapons ban once the Senate agrees to Judge Cavendish's nomination and he's seated. It's looking like the most significant Second Amendment decision since *Hendricks.* With a new justice on the Court, the gun safety people want another swing at *Hendricks.*"

"And your point is?"

"Well, do you want to have another talk with Judge Cavendish before he faces the Senate? See where he might go on the Missouri case?"

"You're thinking we might want to yank the nomination if Cavendish doesn't agree with us on guns?"

"It's an explosive issue, Ma'am, one that could divide the country more than it is already and threaten your presidency."

"Do you think he'd agree to a sit down at this point, so close to the hearings? That would seem to be political, would it not?"

"Not sure. He's a strange duck. Independent-minded. He might go along with it. I have a hunch he doesn't see himself as political. It might work."

"How do we approach him?"

"Possibly through one of Rhode Island's senators. It is not out of the ordinary for a nominating president to re-interview the candidate."

"Forget those senators. I want you to set it up. I want to get it out of the way before next week."

"Right away."

♠

McKinnon stopped at Quach's desk after closing the door to the Oval.

"Okay, Stephanie. There's a florist shop in Yorktown, Indiana, that makes the race winner's wreath each year."

Quach was scribbling notes.

"Well, I should have said there's a female florist in Yorktown who does it. White orchids. That would be appropriate … Oops! Wait a second. Agabashian never won the race. So, on second thought, a combination of white carnations and red roses would be better. Okay? Wouldn't make it seem we were pushing something that never happened."

Quach looked up and nodded.

♠

EIGHT

A well-regulated Militia, being necessary to the security of a free State, the right of the people to keep and bear Arms, shall not be infringed.

The president and the attorney general met for lunch in the President's Private Dining Room on the second floor of the White House. President Addison included McKinnon and the attorney general his chief of staff, Moira Stewart.

The room had a checkered history, thanks mostly to a series of First Ladies with very different ideas about home décor. Some—no one has said who among them—may have employed principals of Feng Shui.

As a waiter filled their water glasses, Jordan began the conversation. He may have done so to delay the true reason for the luncheon.

"Madam President, Moira's been telling me a bit about this room," he said as he opened his napkin and moved it to his lap. "It's very interesting and quite astonishing."

"That's terrific, Moira. I'm listening carefully."

"Well, Madam President, the first thing to say is that for most of its existence it was a bedroom! Its modern form began in 1952 when the Trumans wanted major architectural changes to the White House generally and specifically the Lincoln Bedroom, as people knew this room then, and a series of First Ladies made more changes to the room over the years. Much of that was about the choice of wallpaper or paint. Today it's much like it was under President Kennedy."

"This was the famous Lincoln Bedroom? Everyone's heard of that room, probably more than any room other than the Oval Office. We're eating on Lincoln's bed?"

The four of them laughed.

"To finish the story," Moira continued, "First Lady Jacqueline Kennedy transformed the Lincoln Bedroom into the President's Dining Room. She felt the Family Dining Room on the state floor, which is another name for the first floor, was too cavernous and impersonal for a young family and decided the second floor could support a smaller, more intimate dining room. There you have it! A new Family Dining Room."

♠

"That's terrific! Moira," Addison complimented her guest. Then she turned to the staff person serving them.

"That's fine, Ruth. I'll ring when we're ready for the entrée."

She waited for the staff to finish serving the salad course and clear the room.

"Now we move from the sublime … should I say it … to the ridiculous. Simon, I want to know about the *Hendricks* decision, so I have some basis on which to question our nominee without showing myself to be a complete dope."

"Its official title is *Leavenworth, Washington v. Hendricks.* The Court decided it by 6–3. It was the most important challenge to the Second Amendment in a half-century."

Addison looked at her chief of staff.

"I'm taking notes," Sean reassured her.

"Should I go on?"

"Yes, of course, Simon."

"Nine pro-gun residents of the city of Leavenworth asked the District Court to enjoin enforcement of three provisions of the city's Firearms Safekeeping & Regulations Act that generally banned the registration of handguns, prohibited the carrying of unlicensed handguns or any other 'deadly or dangerous' weapon capable of concealment, and required that owners disassemble lawfully stored firearms or lock them to prevent firing …

"These nine were the *plaintiffs* …

"The city asked the District Court to dismiss the pro-gun request to stop the enforcement of the Safekeeping & Regulations Act, and it complied ...

"The city was the *defendant* …

"How're we doing so far, Madam President?"

"Great! Simon, thanks."

"The next step was the involvement of the Ninth Circuit Court of Appeals. We'll call it an *appellate* court. That court determined only one of the plaintiffs, Paul Hendricks, had standing to sue, as only he had suffered an injury (arrested for possession of an unlicensed shotgun in a public place), and it struck down the entire law. The city filed for certiorari (relief) directly to the Supreme Court ...

"A slim majority of justices held first that the Second Amendment guaranteed an individual right to possess firearms, independent of service in a state militia; and second to keep firearms for traditionally lawful purposes, including home defense ...

"This meant the majority had endorsed the so-called 'individual-right' theory of the Second Amendment's meaning and rejected a rival interpretation, the 'collective-right' theory. The government argued the latter protected the right of states to maintain militias, and individuals had the right to keep and bear arms *in connection with service in a militia* …

"Let's call that the first legal argument. Still good?"

"Still good, Simon.

Sean continued the scribble furiously.

"Okay. The majority held that the Second Amendment's preamble, '*A well-regulated Militia, being necessary to the security of a free State*,' was consistent with their interpretation. It concluded the framers' believed the most effective way to destroy a citizens' militia was to disarm the citizens …

"Let's call that the amendment's *preamble*, which is half of the second legal argument."

"So," Addison interrupted, "the majority seems to have recognized that bearing arms related to militia service."

"That's one way to look at it."

"Sean?"

"I'm good, Simon."

"Excellent! However, writing for the majority, Mateo Ricci argued that the *operative clause* of the amendment, '*the right of the people to keep and bear Arms, shall not be infringed*,' guaranteed an individual right found in English common law ...

"Finally, the Court held that, because the framers understood the right of self-defense to be "the *central component*" of the right to keep and bear arms, the Second Amendment implicitly protected the right "to use arms in defense of hearth and home."

"Whoa! Whoa! Whoa! That seems like a huge leap. Isn't there a difference between individual self-defense and collective defense? The amendment says nothing about individual self-defense but specifically addresses collective defense, right?"

"It has seemed so to some, Madam President ...

"In his dissenting opinion, Justice Tobias Allen asserted that the Court's decision 'failed to identify any new evidence that the Amendment was intended to limit the power of Congress to regulate civilian uses of weapons." He criticized the Court for attempting to 'denigrate' the importance of the preamble by ignoring its disambiguation of the operative clause."

"Whoa! Whoa! Whoa! What the hell is this 'disambiguation'?"

"More than one meaning, or the problem of resolving syntactic ambiguity. Allen meant that Ricci 'denigrated' the meaning of the preamble by pretending it had no relationship to his operative clause. Okay?"

"Yes, I think so."

"Justice Joseph Silverman added a separate opinion, accepted later by scores of 'inferior courts' as *the* collective-right view of the Second Amendment."

Sean cleared his throat.

"Okay, okay, Simon. I think I got *Hendricks*. Is there more I should know? I've got a four o'clock."

"I'll send you a memo with some talking points that you can use or not use with Cavendish. Thank you for the lunch and conversation, Madam President. Nice to see you, Sean," the attorney general said as he stood to leave.

"Moira, I hope to see you again, soon. Maybe we should have a 'girls only' lunch."

"That would suit me, Madam President," but Moira knew the suggestion was one of those polite "let's have lunch sometime" invites that was never meant to happen.

S-E-C-R-E-T

OFFICE OF THE ATTORNEY GENERAL

Memorandum

TO: President Gloria Addison

FROM: Simon Jordan, Attorney General

CC: Sean McKinnon, Chief of Staff to the President; Moira Stewart, Chief of Staff to the Attorney General

SUBJECT: Second Amendment talking points

Madam President: A quick reminder at the outset. I expect Judge Cavendish to tell you that any discussion between the two of you on this topic is inappropriate. I also have no doubt you will have an adequate response.

In general, the debate over guns runs along a familiar vein of American history: the interest of the individual versus the interest of the community, which we pretend are not entwined. We create contrasts, I believe, to empower one party over another with no acknowledgment of the symbiotic relationship between the individual and the collective.

American political parties, which are more alike than not, thrive on false dichotomies; you are not supposed to like the other guys, and gals, and so, you don't.

♠

Wishful thinkers say the Founders were too intelligent to have made a suicide pact of the Constitution. I'm afraid, however, they did. I think of it as the illogic of the Constitution. The first attempted suicide nearly succeeded between 1861 and 1865, thanks to the myopic vision of the Founders who decided, to get their Constitution ratified, the country could survive with slavery.

We now find ourselves on the precipice of another civil war, one that will still be based on geography but far more deadly than the first. This time there will be no Lincoln to save us from ourselves.

A well-regulated Militia, being necessary to the security of a free State, the right of the people to keep and bear Arms, shall not be infringed.

Consider the following:

1. The Second Amendment is unclear to some, a problem of disambiguation, to use a word from Justice Allen's dissent in *Hendricks*, and that's the problem. While stating the need for a 'well-regulated Militia,' does it guarantee, *as a separate matter*, the right of individuals (people) to 'keep and bear arms'? *Doesn't the second clause depend on the first?* That would seem to be the central conundrum.

The opening clause of the Second Amendment is the *elephant in the room*, the issue everyone is aware of but nevertheless ignores because they find discussion of the clause uncomfortable. It's uncomfortable because the recognition of it, taking it seriously, would undermine their argument for an unfettered individual right to 'keep and bear' arms.

If the Framers really wanted everyone to have a gun, why didn't they come right out and say so? But the Framers didn't write it in a way that said so, which would have been evident had they separated the two clauses with a semi-colon.

Nor did they use the word person, as if referring to individuals, as they did in the Fifth Amendment, which states 'No person shall be held to answer for a capital . . . crime . . . ,' etc. Instead, the only two subjects in the Second Amendment are collective nouns: 'state Militia' and 'people.' Where, then, can anyone find an individual right to own a weapon except as part of a 'well-regulated Militia'?

2. The Second Amendment was one of nineteen original Amendments suggested by the thirteen State Legislatures and compiled (and rewritten) by James Madison, who offered them to Congress in 1791 as part of the Bill of Rights. And most important, this is how James Madison first wrote it:

'The right of the people to keep and bear arms shall not be infringed, a well-armed and well-regulated militia being the best security of a free

country; but no person religiously scrupulous of bearing arms shall be compelled to render military service in person.'

Madison's intent could not be more obvious: the Second Amendment refers only to state militias and military service. If not, why include that exemption for what we now call conscientious objectors?

A joint committee from the House and Senate lopped off the religious exemption as too cumbersome in language and too complex to enforce. Thus, the amendment as it now stands. But Madison's Original Intent remains and is there hiding in plain sight for any Supreme Court Justice who takes the pains to look for it.

3. While considering words and their meaning, reflect on the phrase 'to bear arms.' The common usage of 'bearing arms' is in a strictly military (militia) context. To 'order arms' is a military expression.

Americans who owned guns in 1787 and were not part of a militia didn't say of themselves that they '*bore*' arms, and they don't say so today. They carry, tote, lug, clutch, or hold weapons.

They also don't bear '*arms*.' They carry a weapon, a piece, a rifle, a gun, a gat, a heater, heat, a rod, a pistol, a revolver, a handgun, a Saturday night special.

Any man who has been through basic training in the military has heard and memorized the marching ditty: 'This is my rifle; this is my gun. This one's for killin'; this one's for fun.'

4. The pro-gun people ignore, as well, the very reason the Second Amendment got into the Constitution in the first place: to calm the anti-Federalists' fears of the establishment of a standing army. The Second Amendment is, in fact, Madison's (and the

Federalists') response to those who felt threatened that the strong central government, as proposed in the new Constitution, might disarm the state militias. To miss that connection is to miss everything.

5. As written, the Second Amendment follows closely in meaning and language previous state and national constitutions, all of which explicitly refer to militias and not individuals. The Articles of Confederation, the U.S. plan that preceded the ratification of the Constitution, put it this way:

> *"Every State shall always keep up a well-regulated and disciplined Militia, sufficiently armed and accoutered, and shall provide and consistently have ready for use in Public stores, a due number of field pieces and tents, and a proper quantity of arms, ammunition and camp equipage."*

6. Only one of the thirteen state Constitutions, Pennsylvania's, granted the right of individual ownership:

> *'The people have a right to bear arms for the defense of themselves and their own state, or the United States, or for the purpose of killing game; and no law shall be passed for disarming the people or any of them, unless for crimes committed, or real danger of public injury from individuals; and as standing armies in the time of peace are dangerous to liberty, they ought not to be kept up: and that the military shall be kept under strict subordination to and be governed by the civil powers.'*

Pennsylvania proved the exception because of its western settlers who feared Native American attacks almost as much as they despised Quakers back east who hated guns. Note that the state allowed disarmament in cases of 'real danger of public injury from individuals.'

7. Madame President, the following point may be one of your best weapons with the Judge:

The Founders limited freedom whenever it clashed with *public safety*. Neither the delegates to the Constitutional Convention, the Congressional debates of 1791, nor The Federalist discussed, debated, voted on, or even mentioned individual gun rights. Guns may have been part of American life, but as far as a man's right to own one of them, the Constitution is silent.

And here's the evidence:

a) Jefferson—writing to Madison from Paris about the Bill of Rights—only talks about the State's 'protection against Standing Armies.'

b) The Library of Congress database containing the official records of all debates in the United States at that time, includes thirty uses of the phrase 'to bear arms.' In every one of those uses, the phrase has an unambiguous military meaning.

c) In a National Archive search of the database of all the writings of Washington, Adams, Franklin, Hamilton, and Madison, the term 'bear arms' produces 153 mentions—all in a military context (see also; No. 3 above).

8. The Founders were afraid of guns in the wrong hands. Not just slaves. Not just Native Americans. But *angry white men* (Shay's Rebellion). The Second Amendment ('shall not be infringed') is a contradiction of—overturns—the following existing restrictions and others of a similar nature:

a) It was *illegal* in Boston (1787) to keep a loaded gun in your house.

b) All states *prohibited* people considered dangerous from owning a weapon.

c) A Boston statute (1786) called for the safe storage of gunpowder within the city limits and allowed for the town's fire wardens to *confiscate* weapons for violations of that law.

9. In *Hendricks*, Justice Mateo Ricci sublimated his boastful originalism to an ill-disguised political sycophancy. His view of the Second Amendment was not an illumination of the wisdom of the Founders but instead a paean to the moneyed power of the National Rifle Association.

He ignored:

a) two hundred years of precedent,

b) historical context,

c) the plain meaning of words,

d) the Framers' intent,

e) and the D.C. laws of its elected officials to focus solely on the text of the Second Amendment,

f) which he arbitrarily separated into two parts, ignoring the clear, intentional symbiosis of the two clauses, as noted.

Disambiguous. Deceitful. Disgraceful. Destructive.

♠

Finally, I would offer the NRA people the following proposition to demonstrate the inappropriate comparison of the time of the incorporation of the Second Amendment to today's arms.

Build a model human from the most flesh-like material we have. Get a musket, vintage 1780s, and fire on the dummy from say 10 feet to 10 yards distant. Then get an AR-15 style rifle and do the same. I daresay the result will be dramatically different!

♠

> My personal view about guns is well known. I have made it clear throughout most of my private and public life that should we continue down the path we are on, one in which the current view of the Second is considered more important than the lives of our children—the life of anyone—sooner rather than later the Second Amendment will bring about the end of the United States as we know it.

♠

The president pressed Stephanie's intercom button. Thirty seconds later she stood before the *Resolute* desk.

"I've got a pressing job for you," the president began. "Can you put aside the other stuff for an hour or two, or however long this might take?"

Stephanie Quach knew she could not possibly be too busy when the president put it like that.

"Yes, of course, Madam President."

"I want you to take this memo from Mr. McKinnon, pick out *only* the points he raises about the Second, type that up on my stationery as a letter to Judge Cavendish, and bring it back for me to go over. I'll edit it for a final draft. Got it?"

"Absolutely, Madam President!"

A half hour later Stephanie had prepared a draft using Jordan's central points but omitting his personal views. She brought it to the president.

"Okay, let's have it," she said.

She stalled.

"Stephanie?"

She stalled because she was about to present something to the President of the United States that perhaps she ought not. She could feel her buttocks tightening.

"Well? I haven't got all day, Stephanie. What have you got? Out with it!"

"Madam President, are you sure you want me to send this letter?"

"What! Let me see that."

She rocked forward in her huge recliner and reached across the *Resolute* toward Stephanie's outstretched hand holding the letter.

"Thanks, Stephanie."

♠

The President

of the United States

The White House

1600 Pennsylvania Ave.

Washington D.C., 20500

June 23

Hon. Judge Randolph Cavendish
District of Columbia Court of Appeals

Dear Judge Cavendish ...

Gloria took a few minutes to look over the draft. Finally, she looked up.

"This looks terrific, Stephanie. I don't see the need for any changes. Please bring me a final copy for signature."

"Will there be anything else, Madam President?"

"No, Stephanie," she smiled. "Great job on the letter! Bring me the final then skedaddle! I'll see you tomorrow."

♠

TEN

The insistent ringing of Paul Vanni's cell phone woke him unpleasantly from a deep sleep. After a few moments spent struggling to gather his wits, he raised his head to check the digital clock radio on the nightstand next to his bed: 4:45 A.M.

'What the f**k!'

The ringing continued, hammering away at his brain. The phone was a 'burner,' a throwaway, untraceable. So, no voicemail to end the ringing that was driving him mad. He also questioned why he kept the damn thing near his bed in the first place, and why the idiot at the other end hadn't given up after three or four rings.

When he had finally managed to clear the fog in his head and look at the phone, it read simply, 'potential spam.'

"F**k! he shouted at the phone, peeved that some spanner woke him so rudely, but it would have been nothing more than a disembodied voice at the other end.

He did, however, recognize the Washington, D.C. area code.

♠

Paolo Vanni was second-generation Italian. His parents, Anita and Giovanni, with Paolo's two older sisters and three brothers in tow, part of the great Italian diaspora of the 1920s, left Italy for good from Lucca, a poverty-stricken town in the northern province of Tuscany. Paolo was born two years later in the Italian ghetto of New York City known as 'Little Italy.'

Young Paolo grew up learning how to con the unsuspecting and skirt the law. Those techniques were just what kids from the lower class of neighborhoods of 'Little Italy' learned they must do to earn respect and survive.

He toyed with school and dropped out when he reached sixteen, despite everything Anita Vanni tried to change the direction of this life. It seemed to Paolo that his mother worried endlessly about everything, and his father struggled to provide for his large family. He decided two things at a tender age at home and on the tough streets of 'Little Italy': one, never marry, thereby avoiding a large family's drain on resources; and two, discover moneymaking paths his father hadn't, legitimate or not.

Paolo eventually discovered he couldn't perpetually escape the long arm of the government. Drafted in late 1944, the young ne'er-do-well who now went by Paul, wound up in an infantry unit the following spring advancing up the western slope of the Apennines. The terrain was impossibly difficult, especially for a private who had known only the flat streets of 'Little Italy.' The clever delaying tactics of the retreating Germans provided an even more difficult challenge for the American Fifth Army.

Somewhere in the Po Valley a mortar blast put Paul in a field hospital located only a few kilometers from Lucca. When Giovanni learned of his son's location in a telegram from the War Department, he contacted family in Lucca through the Red Cross. Before Paul heard of his father's intervention, the local family had descended on the hospital and laid siege to their relative's bedside. Every convalescing soldier should be so lucky!

♠

Stateside and free of hospitalization, therapy, and the Army itself, Paul fell under the sway of other young Italian-American men. All were graduates of the mean streets of 'Little Italy,' whose central issue of life was the conviction that the elites who ran the country had discriminated against them in jobs, society, and politics. These resourceful young men, unemployed and well-trained by Uncle Sam in the techniques and usefulness of violence, made it their life's work to create and support a close-knit, secretive family that could care for its members when others couldn't or wouldn't, regardless of who stood in the way.

And what would separate him from the ranks of those who stood in his way? Guns. Vanni's slide into the world of guns and his efforts to court the small circle of men who hired themselves out to commit murder. Paul Vanni became a hit man. Laughably so, it turned out.

♠

It began quite by accident, as such changes in a man's life often did. His landlady, a seemingly charming woman named Helen Grills, who turned out to be anything but charming, came to him with a complaint about a deadbeat renter. She had been impressed with Vanni's physical appearance rather than his depressed mind, the reason for which she knew nothing and couldn't have cared less.

She had an agenda that required his attention, depressed or not. Would he pay the deadbeat a visit on her behalf? Threaten him in some fashion? She said it'd be worth a month's rent if he could. He'd always liked her. He liked the attention she gave him, liked feeling important. So, he agreed.

It did not go well. The deadbeat balked; Vanni pressed. The deadbeat tried to push Vanni out the door; Vanni pushed back. The deadbeat pulled a switchblade; a mistake for which he would pay dearly. Vanni, remembering his Army training, kicked the man in the groin, which sent the knife flying.

Doubled over in pain, the deadbeat tried to retrieve the knife from the floor, two to three feet distant, but Vanni got there first. On his knees, he grabbed the knife, and with one swift and powerful upward thrust he did to the deadbeat what he'd never been close enough to do to a German soldier. He moved quickly away from the man's falling body and his spurting blood.

He sat next to the body for a few minutes, collecting his thoughts and formulating a plan. He concluded he was probably safe; the only person who knew he'd been there was the landlady. He wiped down the knife to remove his fingerprints. He smiled when he thought of the chagrined fingerprint expert who would come up empty.

The killer rummaged through the man's pockets for his wallet. From his driver's license he made a mental note of the man's name in the event he later read something about the crime. He left with all the man's money and the knife still protruding from his chest.

"What happened?" Grills asked as Paul counted out her missing rent money.

"He resisted and pulled a knife. I just did what the Army trained me to do."

That ended her curiosity.

He neglected to mention to his 'client' that he had pocketed the rest of the man's money as a fee, his first!

♠

Paul Vanni was adjusting to his métier. He possessed great power without seeming to have power at all. Murder for hire. He'd capitalize on the image of himself as a loser in disguise. Who would ever suspect such a person?

Unfortunately, some did. The so-called 'deadbeat' was not that at all. He was a mobster on the lam, on whom a contract had been put out. Word quickly spread of his demise. But who had jumped the legitimate contract? Two who intended to find out descended on the landlady. It required little imagination to guess how long it took for her to give up Paul Vanni. Word quickly spread among mobsters and their contractors or 'assets' that there was a new, unidentified player in town, who now became, in a cruel irony, the subject of a 'contract' himself.

Vanni went on the lam, hiding from the 'contract,' desperately trying to avoid exposure lest he wind up like his victim. His mistake had been to stiff the one person who posed the least danger to him: his landlady.

The reputation of the man on whom a contract existed but had little or no record as a serious professional grew, not only among the criminal element but, oddly, among the country's elites, those with scores to settle lest they lose money and power—even their lives. Perhaps the underworld and the elites—the same, said some—were more entwined than law enforcement imagined.

A potential client—presumably the person who made that early morning call—who had need of someone unlikely to be known by law enforcement because of his lack of 'jobs,' wanted to meet Vanni and size him up.

♠

He'd had a rough night with fitful sleep and nightmares that seemed unrelated to him. Then came that call, which really worried him. Not so much the call itself, but the person at the other end. How had the caller learned Paul's name and especially his number? Who had recommended him? He'd never done business with anyone at this man's level of power. Was he being set up? If so, by whom?

Paul realized only one person had been close enough to him to provide his name and number: Helen Grills.

'Sonofabitch!'

Maybe she'd seen the phone's number when he left in on a table or chair or somewhere. Did he give it to her when he rented? All guesses. He ought to pay her a visit, he thought, but he was clever enough to know if he showed up there, he'd be a walking dead man. The dead-beat renter's associates would be watching the place. He had no idea, of course, that there had been a contract on the man. That would have meant even greater danger. So, he'd continue to lie low and wait for developments come to him.

Yeah, it had been a rough night.

ELEVEN

Paul Vanni may have fancied himself—or was fancied by others—as a hit man of sorts, but he did not fit the familiar mold. A job for one's landlady, an accidental 'hit,' did not a professional reputation make. Moreover, he was not yet 'connected,' despite his ethnic background, not someone motivated by conspiratorial thinking, not someone who carried out vendettas.

There were other stereotypical qualities missing from Vanni's portfolio, absent qualities that might have interested a client with more than a casual interest in still being in the shadows: someone who did his killing in a highly planned, methodical, and organized manner; someone with adept social judgment; and someone with a personality that reflected orderliness, control, and paranoid vigilance. Those gaping holes in his résumé all but guaranteed a man like Paul Vanni would never come to the attention of authorities. Who would bother to look among society's losers for a hit man?

What kind of hit man was Paul Vanni? Where on the scales of ability and accomplishment would one find him? Vanni's first hit (accidental) showed him headed neither up nor down in his new (possibly) profession. Was he a 'novice' (total fledgling)? 'Dilettante' (bumbling idiot who kills without enthusiasm or skill because he's desperate for cash)? 'Journeyman' (far more skilled than the 'novice' but can still flounder in the moment)? Or 'Master' (criminal ability; doesn't commit the same mistakes as others; parachutes in, makes the kill, and leaves immediately)?

One had to admit that he excelled at his 'craft' and 'executed' his contract quietly and without incident. His client meeting took place in secret. He executed the job with precision and grace. And no one saw the escape. Vanni's 'hit' did not show the glamor of films and novels. No smoke-filled rooms, bars, or casinos where gangsters hung out.

Paul's first 'contract' fit other parameters of murder for hire. Most killers selected uninteresting places for their dirty work; just as often the location selected itself, and the killer had no choice in the matter. Killers occasionally bungled the job, and their clients had lame motivations. Most took place for very small sums.

What motivated clients to seek out people like Vanni? Sour business deals or rivalries? Disputes among gang members? Domestic disagreements between divorcing husbands and wives? Cases of mistaken identity? Or hits related to 'honor' killings?

Had Paul Vanni been a true student of his art, he would have learned that most of the hits carried out in his day were committed by the first three categories of killers: the novice, the dilettante, or the journeyman. Their murders, as the categories just mentioned suggested, were 'commonplace and ordinary' in their execution, and 'mundane' in their motives. But, the true student, who wasn't Paul Vanni, as noted, would also have learned, and a prospective client should want to know before hiring Vanni, that there was an important statistical warning to consider: the statistics just cited were of hit men who did not escape the long arm of the law, in which one of several lethal means shortened their earthly time or lengthened it by long prison sentences.

Hit men who remained at large, the 'Masters,' a title that pertained only to unsolved murders, might have presented a very different profile. Hardly commonplace or mundane. There might be some hit men so adept that the death of their victim did not even raise suspicion and were, instead, simply thought the result of natural causes. No one could think the demise of Vanni's first victim resulted from natural causes, but would it go unsolved, making of him a 'half-Master'?

♠

Then, unfinished business. That early morning phone call.

"Who the f**k *are* you? Goddammit, this had better be good! You got any idea what time it is?" he shouted into his phone.

♠

TWELVE

Ralph Donaldson and Randy Cavendish had been buddies at Harvard Law, if one can imagine a friendly relationship between two rich guys of very different backgrounds, one old New England and the other an oil rich Texan from Houston. Yet neither held his status nor, in Ralph's case, his wealth against the other. Regarding the latter, Randy didn't have much skin in the game.

Of course, there had been rumors aplenty to explain the closeness of such a friendship but never any convincing evidence of something others saw as 'unorthodox.'

Ralph was looser than Randy … more than a little … not a 'Type A'. He wasn't loose in any moral sense, just more of a freewheeler. Just go with fun loving and leave the rest to imagination. Of utmost importance to their relationship, however, was that they trusted each other, which was a good thing considering Ralph's proclivity for wandering off the ranch, so to speak. Randy did not share his friend's 'style,' but he admired Ralph's challenges, his chutzpah, to the kind of good order bred into Randy. The latter understood the necessity for stasis, but he often itched, philosophically, to give it a good scratch.

Although private practice did not interest Randy, the obscenely oil-rich Ralph added millions to his portfolio from his work at a large firm. It might seem a little odd, then, that Randy would place a call to his Texas buddy on a matter of extreme importance and sensitivity, a man given to, shall we say, sashaying right up to the line of illegality (chutzpah)—an excellent lawyer, Ralph knew precisely where that line existed—and ask for his opinion on an ethical matter. But Randolph Cavendish did place the call, and the reason behind it Ralph would find wholly unexpected and astonishing—eventually.

♠

"Hello, ol' pal!" Donaldson practically shouted.

Cavendish was preparing to reply when the Houston attorney cut him off in an abrupt change of tone.

"You on a secure line?"

"I don't think so, why?"

"Hang up and call me back after you get one of those ten-dollar phones at a convenience store. Electronic retailers will sell prepaid SIM cards and burner phones.

Try Walmart, Best Buy, Target, other places like those—7 Eleven, RiteAide—you got the idea."

With that, Donaldson hung up, leaving his friend literally speechless.

'What a naïve SOB,' Donaldson muttered to himself. 'Nominated to the Supreme Court; awaiting hearings that will certainly be contentious, staff looking for dirt everywhere imaginable; and my pal doesn't realize they're going to be listening to everything he says.'

Cavendish knew he needed help.

"Linda," Cavendish immediately called out to his executive assistant who occupied an adjoining office. "What's a 'burner phone'? Someone just asked me to get one and call him back."

Linda Shields had worked for Randy Cavendish for years, certainly prior to his accension to the Appeals Court. Like any good executive assistant at that level, she needed—and had—more common sense than her boss (street smarts, a missing quality in too many judges); some who knew both thought she had more brains—period. She also possessed something akin to a mother's protective instinct for her child when she believed Cavendish was somehow threatened.

Linda slouched back in her chair and looked up quizzically at Cavendish.

"Do you mind my asking if this is about the call that you just made?"

"Yes, it was to an old law school buddy. He's in a big Houston firm. He asked if the line were secure … before I said anything!"

She gave him a serious stare.

"Various people in many ways have expressed this, 'God has a special providence for fools, drunkards, and the United States of America,' said Chancellor Otto von Bismarck,' and Leo Durocher came up with this one: 'God watches over drunks and third basemen,' and I am going to join them by appending an addition.

She smiled and they both laughed.

"Alright, alright, I know what your addition would be."

"Okay, then. Respectfully, sir, it's time to think about the ramifications of your nomination to the Supreme Court—the Supreme Court! A lot of people have a 'supreme' interest in the outcome. They will be looking for dirt, even where it can't possibly exist. So, from now on no calls in or out except on the 'burner.'"

"Okay, but tell me about a 'burner.'"

"A burner phone is a cheap, prepaid mobile phone that the owner, that's you, purchased with cash to avoid a paper trail that would tie the phone number to an individual. Once you suspect someone can trace the phone to you, discard or 'burn' it ...

"But remember this. No cell phone provides true anonymity. Here's a hypothetical ...

"Let's say that you drive to a store, buy the burner phone with a credit card, drive home, and turn it on. If you took your normal phone with you, your cellular carrier would know you were at the store when you purchased the phone. A camera in the store may have recorded you buying the phone. Your credit card company will have a record of your purchase. And here's a real possibility. if you carry your burner phone and normal phone at the same time, both on, anyone looking at cellular phone records can get a pretty good idea you own both phones ...

"You could ask someone else to buy it for you or ask them to purchase a gift card for you. You could also use cash in person. You should avoid using your credit or debit card. Do NOT buy one online!"

"Linda, here's fifty dollars. Can you please make the purchase for me? It's very important I call my friend."

"Of course, Judge. I can do it on my lunch break."

'I saw that one coming a mile away!' she muttered quietly as he walked toward his office. 'He needs a wife.'

He stopped at the open door separating their offices.

"Linda, please take all the time you need and more to get that phone. Don't cut short your lunch break to do it ...

"I have a better idea. When you return, we'll spend what's left of the afternoon in my learning how to use it. How does that sound?"

"I can live with it, but I don't believe it'll take all afternoon for you to get comfortable with the phone."

He smiled.

"I'll see you when you return from lunch, Linda. By the way, where do you go for lunch?"

"Usually, Mangialardo's, just up from the Potomac Metro stop. It's primarily subs … inexpensive and quick."

"Terrific! Thanks."

♠

THIRTEEN

Randolph Cavendish proved an apt pupil. Either that or Linda Shields was an even better teacher. At any rate, the afternoon 'burner' lesson went smoothly, and Judge Cavendish looked forward to making that advisory call to his friend the next morning. He couldn't wait for Ralph to ask again if the line was secure. Judge Randolph Cavendish was ready to sound like an expert! The business about a 'burner' phone, however, should not cloud or minimize the seriousness of Cavendish's reason for the call.

The phone was only a means to an end, that end being Cavendish's meeting with the president. One might imagine the president made certain assumptions about her nominee, just as Cavendish had of her. It did not bode well. Cavendish was no waif in the run-up to confirmation. He was not unaware the president wanted more from him than an introductory meeting filled with insincere platitudes out of both their mouths and the rest small talk. He wasn't wrong.

That the president might believe she could cleverly disguise her intent; the judge would not know what she wanted from him. That would be a shocking degree of arrogance. The president's conceit amounted to an ill-conceived, ill-concealed, and ill-executed ambush. Cavendish would not know what hit him!

This the nominee did not know the precise agenda of his meeting with the president, but he was clever enough to anticipate what might happen. He might imagine, for instance, that to carry out the administration's plan Attorney General Jordan had advised President Addison to learn which of Judge Cavendish's past opinions he felt comfortable in discussing. Once that door opened, even by a crack, the challenge for the president would be to move the conversation from there to his view of the Second Amendment. Addison would need to do so with sufficient subtlety to prevent the nominee from realizing Addison was instructing him how, if confirmed by the Senate, he should rule on any gun case before the Court.

'She wants this meeting because she takes me for a fool, a tool, and herself a genius. What chutzpah!'

It was in that frame of mind that Randolph Cavendish picked up his disposable phone and called his old friend.

♠

"Ralphie? Randy here."

"Did you take care of that problem we discussed yesterday?"

"Sure did. You doin' the same?"

"Soon as I saw who was calling. I transferred you from the office land line to my 'special phone.' So, what's on your mind, ol' pal?"

"Well, this is gonna kill you. It's an ethical question."

Silence.

"You gonna have me disbarred if I don't give you the 'right' answer?"

Randy laughed.

"Wait! You haven't heard the question yet."

"Knowing you, it'll be a doozy."

"Seriously, Ralphie, I've got a bit of a dilemma about this nomination. It involves the president."

"Oh, f**k, Randy! I can tell you right now that whatever it is with the president, don't go there. I've heard stuff."

Silence.

"Heard what?"

Silence.

"Accidents. Suicides."

"Come on, Ralphie! You gotta explain that."

"There's nothing concrete. Coincidences. Circumstantial evidence."

"Of what?"

"Those accidents and suicides. People that cross her. People who don't cooperate. Stuff has happened to them way out of proportion to accidents and suicides in the general population."

"And you know this how?"

"CI's. FOX News."

"I might begin believe it when someone shows up on '60 Minutes.'"

"Just watch your back. That's all I'm sayin.' So, what's this call about? Some ethical issue, you said."

"She wants to meet and talk judicial philosophy, I suppose. Probably my opinions and rulings. Fishing expedition. Can she trust me to deliver, et cetera, et cetera?"

"Well, Randy, it's within the world of expectation that the president who nominates a justice ought to have confidence in, or an expectation of, how they would rule in certain cases. Abortion, free speech, school prayer, guns—the usual gamut. I sense you've got a problem with this conference, otherwise it might be another six months before I heard from you again."

"I know we're from the same party and political persuasion, the president and me, but my gut tells me she's up to something."

"Well, go to the interview and find out. Can't hurt. But before it starts, tell her you'll need a stenographic copy of the interview. See how she reacts to that. Talk as little as possible. Keep your opinions close to the vest. Listen. Get a sense where she's headed. As for the ethical question, I don't see one. Maybe she'll say something that will be problematic. Watch for it and get in touch afterwards."

"Thanks, Ralphie. You've been kind to listen and provided plenty for me to consider. I feel better about the meet but not about those coincidences you mentioned earlier."

"Like I said, watch your back … Listen, Randy, I've got an appointment waiting, pre-trial discovery. Big money involved. Thanks for the call, though. Let me know how your meet went. Always a pleasure."

"Thanks again, Ralphie."

But Ralph Donaldson had rung off.

Ralph's mention of 'big money' left Randy cold. As for his own circumstance, he didn't feel that he'd gained anything from his friend. He had the feeling throughout the call that Donaldson's attention lay elsewhere—with the pre-trial discovery. Understandable. So, he doubted very much that he'd call Ralph following his meeting with the president. What would it accomplish?

FOURTEEN

Clinton Downey, like President Addison, hailed from Columbus. Without much formal education—he had dropped out of Indiana State after two years—he landed a job selling insurance for the local Farmers Insurance franchise, and found a wife, Clarise. Clinton didn't make enough to support the couple on his own—Clarise Downey worked at K-Mart to keep the creditors at bay—but he developed an ability to talk people into small policies. He was persuasive—up to a point.

Objectively, then, the life of twenty-seven-year-old Clinton Downey hadn't amounted to much that one could consider solid. Rather, his was a void, an empty vessel, into which other influences could pour. Despite moderate success selling insurance, Downey felt left behind, unable to accomplish something in which he could take pride. Something big.

But he couldn't catch a break. Harangued by a media that repeated over and over that he should be afraid: afraid of people of color, afraid of tax increases, afraid of drug side effects, Downey, like many Americans, felt even more insecure. None of those things were his fault. Others possessed the power to instill fear and keep people like him from moving up.

But topping the list of forces bearing down on decent, law-abiding Americans like Clinton Downey was the ultimate fear, a certainty 'they' were coming for his guns. 'They' were cheating him out of the success he deserved. But so long as he had his guns they could never triumph.

♠

Since childhood Clinton Downey had been fascinated with games of chance, which he discovered when the carnival descended on his town each spring, summer, or fall for a few days of fun and fleecing. Downey wasn't interested in the rides that fascinated most children, the 'Tilt-a-Whirl,' Ferris Wheel, merry-go-round, or bumper cars. No, tossing balls at plastic tenpins to win a 'Kewpie Doll' or stuffed animal; shooting free throws at a basket placed at an unofficial distance and height; tossing coins at glass jars or numbered squares on a board, the so-called 'penny pitch' for cheap prizes mesmerized Clinton Downey. So easy. One can reasonably imagine that he longed to join the ranks of those who did the fleecing.

It wasn't the skill of the suckers who paid for the

opportunity to win that intrigued Downey. No, what appealed to the young man was how easily a marginal salesman could separate the suckers from their cash at odds so stacked the House couldn't possibly lose.

Downey's world consisted of three groups: the powerful who kept people like him down, the masses of suckers who didn't realize how the powerful disadvantaged them, and a few people like himself clever enough to see through it all. It sure didn't require a college degree to divest the suckers, he would say. The suckers were the ones who thought that degree invaluable. He'd show them!

Possibly there were people that fit Downey's definition of all-seeing beings, but, in truth, he wasn't among them. From age seventeen to the present, Richard Downey had spent what vacation time allotted him, usually no more than a week, finding a nearby carny and working his stand of several game variations, which he lovingly put up and took down before returning to selling insurance.

Importantly, Downey failed to fully appreciate that the suckers weren't all his; yes, he coaxed their interest and raked in their cash. But the 'carny' bosses controlled their vendors (Downey) like a mob protection racket. Their cut—enforced by hulking bodyguards—their 'interest rate,' their payoff, would embarrass even the crassest loan shark. The result? Clinton Downey never got ahead. In time, he came to understand he had become one of the suckers. Parties known or unknown had stacked the deck. They took the big money and left guys like Downey the crumbs—'careers' in jobs that couldn't support a family.

How to account for Downey's infatuation and behavior? He was a grown man with a respectable job, even though he wasn't much good at it. There seemed no satisfactory explanation. Some things don't have explanations that fit the spectrum of rationality. It just was.

On a personal level, Clinton Downey carried with him a basketful of negative qualities. Often unpleasant, he wore a perpetual scowl. He yelled at children at play, considering them a nuisance. Come Halloween, Downey's place became the scene of revenge exacted on a man scorned. When the kids said to him, 'Trick or Treat,' they meant 'Trick.' They rang his doorbell incessantly and soaped his car windows.

"Beat it, you little bastards!" he'd yell, although he toned down the word 'bastards.'

"Up yours," came the cry back from the dark. If one listened closely, they might hear some giggling. In the kids' eyes the word 'curmudgeon' fit Downey to a 'T'; he deserved everything they gave him.

It wasn't just kids and that ever-present scowl. Downey routinely tried to underwrite policies prospective clients didn't need, and when they balked, he raised his voice. He called the local newspaper at least once a week to vent his grievances at whoever answered until that person realized who was on the other end and hung up. Poor Clarise Downey. She couldn't understand the reasons for any of the vitriol directed at her husband.

Finally, a brainstorm! Downey decided that if he ran successfully for a seat on the county board of commissioners, he would have a guaranteed platform for the obvious attention his public acting out craved. Alas, like most things in Downey's life it didn't work out. Following the flop at his only attempt at officeholding, he refused to accept his lopsided loss to Gloria Addison and what he called her distortions about his character during their race.

Now, 'that woman,' an expression he frequently used when speaking to anyone willing to listen to his bombast—also an obvious violation of the canons of successful salesmanship—'that woman' was President of the United States. He never ceased railing about her continuing political success. Her election to national office caused Downey to become menacingly despondent, believing he alone was responsible for her elevation and whatever she did as president.

What might she do, in his opinion? Doubtless, anything she wanted, but he was especially fearful of one imagined objective.

♠

Clinton Downey was a lifetime member of the National Rifle Association and a diehard believer that the Second Amendment bestowed an unqualified right on every American to keep and bear arms. Frankly, Downey had only a vague sense of 18th century 'militias,' or more importantly what militias in his century had to do with the right of citizens to bear arms. He'd read the amendment over and over, heard all the NRA lectures, read all the organization's literature, and for the life of him couldn't understand what all the fuss was about. It says right there, he'd cajole, as plain as the nose on your face (he often went for folksy when wrapping up a potential client), *'the right of the people to keep and bear Arms, shall not be infringed.'* Got nothing to do with militias. Never understood why the author of the Second said anything about them.

He got arguments now and then, but mostly the people who heard his spiel remained silent. Unlike Downey, they found the wording of the amendment confusing. Rather than dismiss talk of militias, most of them tried to make sense of the two clauses—how they fit together.

On one occasion, a clean-cut young man told Downey that since a person had the right to keep and bear arms as part of a militia, the gunowners of America must belong to a government militia …

"Bullshit," Downey yelled.

"*Bear arms* means they have to join the Army," the young man continued, and "get their asses over to Iraq, or Afghanistan, or wherever the United States is at war."

Clinton Downey punched him in the face before he realized the policy he had issued the young man on a better day contained a clause allowing the policyholder to sue an assailant for damages. On the bright side for Downey, however, it was a very expensive policy because of that clause.

Clarise Downey didn't know how to cope with her husband's obsession. She didn't understand why there had to be a fuss over some old amendment, or why her husband had to be away from home and spend so much of their money going to one NRA gig after another.

She screwed up her courage one day and challenged him after he told her he was off to Milwaukee for another convention.

"We can't afford your running off all the time to those NRA meetings," she said. "Besides, I read that the president of that outfit is a crook."

Well, Clarise Downey didn't have one of those 'sue an assailant' policies to protect her physically or financially for what was coming. Clinton gave her a hard slap across the face, forceful enough to send her tumbling backward over an ottoman. She tried to break her fall by putting both arms behind her, which snapped both her wrists and resulted in compound fractures.

♠

Divorced, Clinton Downey was now free to wrap himself in layers of increasing despair over 'that woman' in the White House, who he now believed was about to take away America's gun rights. He and his fellow intellectual travelers were convinced Addison would get restrictive legislation through Congress and then pack the Supreme Court with justices to reverse the *Hendricks* decision. All very clever. All very plausible to a conspiratorial mind. The idea of President Addison's desire to subvert the Second Amendment and the need to stop her had metastasized in Downey's mind to the level of a dangerous obsession.

♠

FIFTEEN

Philip Clark of Portland, Oregon, a successful lumberman, was a tall, chiseled man with a full head of grayish hair set off by a perfectly trimmed Van Dyke mustache and goatee, led the Senate of the United States by virtue of his party's having a majority and his selection as party leader. To a lay person that would seem to bestow great power in the hands of one man; no legislation reached the floor without his consent.

No matter how imposing his countenance and respected his oratorical and legislative proficiencies, Clark knew better. He knew that to seal Judge Cavendish's confirmation he needed fifty of his party colleagues plus the vice-president to break any 50–50 tie.

Daunting as that challenge promised, it would have been more so had not the other party already abandoned the 60-vote threshold for Supreme Court vacancies, the 'filibuster,' when, a few years earlier they were desperate to assure confirmation of one of their nominees. Thus, the real power in the Senate lay with the minority leader's ability to peel off one or two of Clark's 'yeas,' driving his whip count below fifty.

Clark didn't lament the passing of the filibuster. He considered it a relic of the past put into play decades earlier to protect a minority faction in the Senate that opposed civil rights legislation. The old threshold was gone, but Clark's party was still home to a handful of senators from states where the opposition ruled by large margins. Could he or the minority leader count on the senators from those states? Clark believed there was a better than even chance he could pull it off; the president's nominee was known to lean to the opposition's political philosophy, thereby reducing the minority leader's chances of peeling away any of Clark's senators and derailing the confirmation of Judge Cavendish.

♠

President Gloria Addison faced the dilemma that every chief executive who selects a nominee to the Supreme Court must. The reason or reasons why a president picked any person was never black or white, but the expectation was always that the nominee would adhere, generally, at least, to the president's political views. The president should have confidence in the nominee's observance of that expectation—but not always.

The most notable deviation from the script, a justice who did not appear to stick to party ideology, was Earl Warren, a tanned, handsome, and popular Californian, a former attorney general and governor of that state, and a presidential candidate. President Dwight Eisenhower selected Warren, a celebrated act of presidential genius at the time, to occupy the empty chair of 'Chief.'

Soon, however, Warren led the Court to a unanimous judgment in *Brown v. Board of Education.* Since then, every president desirous of moving the Court in a politically advantageous direction had lived with anxiety, fearful they might have on their résumé an 'Earl Warren' with its predictable political backlash.

In nominating Judge Randolph Cavendish, the president had every expectation she had not plucked another justice from obscurity, a deviant, a turncoat who would wander outside the wire, to borrow a metaphor of the battlefield or the American West. But she needed the nominee's assurance. She came at him with both barrels (pardon the pun).

♠

SIXTEEN

"I asked you here today, Judge … I'm going to be frank, and I hope that doesn't offend you … I asked you here today because I want to know what you believe the Second Amendment says, both as to its current meaning—what the Court ruled in *Hendricks*—and the Founders' original intent ...

"Most of all I want you or anyone to persuade me the Founders intended in that amendment for an 18-year-old kid, a teenager unable to buy a beer in most states, to 'keep and bear' an AR-15—a weapon designed to kill as many people in as short a time as possible—to 'keep and bear' that AR-15 without his participation in a militia, participation laughable on its face."

Cavendish blanched, stunned. Nonetheless, the president continued.

"I want to know how closely our views align, as I believe a president and her nominee must be to persuade those in my party, our party, that we have the same general view. That's only prudent if we are to get you that seat on the Court. Wouldn't you agree, Judge?"

Randolph Cavendish, clearly unsettled by Addison's shocking forthrightness, directness, and, as he saw it, her clumsy transparency, paused before responding.

"Madam President, I would not have expected you to be anything other than frank. I'm not unfamiliar with the politics of these nominations or the emotions that accompany the Second Amendment. I hope in return you will not mind my being equally frank."

"Of course not, Judge Cavendish."

"Respectfully, Madam President, I note the presence of a stenographer in the room. Before leaving, I'm going to insist on a copy of what's said here ...

"Now, as to your being frank. Do you intend to ask me to change whatever I believe the Second Amendment—your invitation mentioned that as the single agenda item—to change whatever *you imagine* I believe the amendment purports to say and to adopt your interpretation? Aside from the ethical issue involved in your asking me to do that, and I pray you are not, what you are suggesting is purely hypothetical. If I agreed to do as you wish, I'd need to reference the facts and arguments of a specific case."

"Whoa! Slow down there, cowboy. I'm darn well going to ask *my* nominee anything I darn well please. That nominee is free to respond or not, which, in the latter case he is also free to withdraw his name from consideration. You got any notion how that would look, Judge? Should you choose to withdraw, do you believe you could out-spin the White House's in explaining your pulling out?"

Cavendish's disbelief only increased.

"Let's forget all about coordination for now, Judge. You just explain to me what that amendment says. I'll chime in when I have a question or a different view."

"Do I have a choice?"

"You want that seat?"

"Very well ... Your reputation for persuasion is well deserved, Madam President."

"Flattery will get you everywhere, Judge!"

Laughter replaced the dueling pistols, so to speak, and the pair got down to the reason for the meeting.

♠

SEVENTEEN

"To begin," Cavendish began, "the Second Amendment consists of a subordinate clause, *A well-regulated Militia, being necessary to the security of a free State*, and so forth."

"Hold on there, Mr. Justice! May I call you Randolph?"

"If you like, Madam President."

He was about to say she could call him 'Randy' but thought better of it considering their relative stations.

"Why do you call it a 'subordinate clause'?" she pressed.

"My best explanation is that it doesn't connote any action. It's merely an introduction to the action clause, although it, too, goes by various names. More on that in a moment."

"You mean to say the so-called action clause means nothing without the 'subordinate' clause. That seems important. Okay. Proceed. It just sounded condescending to call it subordinate. Prejudicial. Dismissive. I happen to believe it's the most important clause of the amendment."

Cavendish didn't try to challenge Addison's view of the relative importance of the two clauses.

"That's interesting, Madam President. Very interesting …

"Back to the main clause, what Justice Ricci called the operative clause, *the right of the people to keep and bear Arms, shall not be infringed* …

"The main clause sounds correct in present-day English. The subordinate clause, however, seems to have something wrong with it. That's because it precedes the main clause, and the two clauses have different subjects. This type of clause fell into disuse around a hundred years ago, it seems reasonable that modern readers would not have a good sense of its grammatical soundness or meaning."

"I have a terrific grasp of its meaning, Randolph!"

"To understand the confusing subordinate clause, we must look at historical examples of the construction. A collection of texts from a particular timespan and region that consists of a balanced mix of personal letters, newspapers, scientific treatises, religious texts and so forth. They can tell us how such clauses changed over time and how they were used, so that modern readers have a better idea of how this grammatical construction shapes the meaning of the amendment ...

"Clauses of this type have had four possible meanings, several of which could overlap. First, they could signal that the event happened *before* the main clause event. This is called a *temporal* usage ...

The temporal reading would show that *whenever* 'A well-regulated Militia" is "necessary to the security of a free State,' then 'the right of the people to keep and bear Arms, shall not be infringed.'"

"That sounds like Ricci."

"Yes, perhaps. May I continue?"

Addison waved her hand in obvious irritation to signal 'yes.'

"The second example, the *conditional*, has always been rare. People used conditional *being*-clauses to make predictions ...

"A conditional interpretation would entail that, *if* 'A well-regulated Militia" is ever "necessary to the security of a free State,' then 'the right of the people to keep and bear Arms, shall not be infringed ...

"The third example also evolved from temporals and could likewise overlap with them. These clauses signaled real-world causation. This is an *external causal* because it refers to a cause and a consequence in the real world ...

"The external causal interpretation would mean that "the right of the people to keep and bear Arms, shall not be infringed" *for the purpose* of 'A well-regulated Militia … necessary to the security of a free State …'

"The fourth type of meaning is an *internal causal,* where the subordinate clause supplies the logical basis, not the real-world cause, for the main clause ...

"The internal causal would indicate that *because it is known* that 'A well-regulated Militia" is 'necessary to the security of a free State,' it is concluded that 'the right of the people to keep and bear Arms, shall not be infringed ...'"

"The temporal, external causal, and internal causal readings are not equally likely. Statistically, the temporal and external causal interpretations are the most probable."

The judge saw the president shifting nervously in her oversized recliner, but he decided to press ahead, regardless.

"Both a temporal and a causal reading would assert that "the right of the people to keep and bear Arms, shall not be infringed" *whenever* a militia was "necessary to the security of a free State". The causal reading would additionally assert that the "right" was for the purpose of the necessary militia, and therefore applied whenever the militia was necessary.

"Hold on there, Randolph. You are inserting a bunch of big, fat biases and deviations from the text. You say 'it is known' they needed a militia for security, and therefore the people could keep and bear arms.

Your so-called internal causal seems not only logical but real-world stuff. There is no 'if a militia is necessary' or no 'whenever a militia is necessary.' The amendment supplies no other reason than militias and security for keeping and bearing arms. Therefore, there is no unqualified right to have firearms. That seems to me to be the most important aspect of the amendment. If you say the amendment supports an unqualified right to own guns, you are also saying the authors of the amendment didn't know what they were talking about. Pretty presumptuous."

"Well, you make good points, Madam President. There is a way to see the validity of it in this way. A temporal or causal relation between the clauses would mean that the main-clause was temporally or *causally contingent* on the subordinate clause, and 'the right of the people to keep and bear Arms, shall not be infringed' would only apply when, or for the purpose of, 'A well-regulated Militia being necessary to the security of a free State.'"

"Exactly!" she crowed.

"Interpreting the main clause while ignoring the subordinate clause would be nonsensical, and certainly contrary to the original intent or understanding of the two clauses."

"Bingo!"

"Hold on, Madam President. When was the militia thought necessary? Did the authors mean occasionally necessary? Necessary during an emergency? Or necessary permanently? If the latter, it follows that the right to bear arms would also be perpetual. That timing, I believe, is an issue for historians, not semanticists. It is also a question whether we should adhere to the founders' opinions or those of present-day theorists."

"By the latter you must have Justice Ricci in mind. He fancied himself an originalist when that's convenient and a 'present-day theorist' when the NRA comes calling."

"I don't disagree completely, but I'd prefer to leave Justice Ricci out of it ...

"The Bill of Rights, like Shakespeare's plays, was not badly written. The Second Amendment was *grammatically correct* and probably *unambiguous* at the time of its writing. Perhaps the process of changes in language has confused the argument—or perhaps it's present-day speakers who have a motive or motives *not* to acknowledge those changes."

"Well, Judge, as you know I invited you here today to get your view of the Second, and I'm not sure I have it."

"Madam President, as you know, Court decisions are based to a large extent on a collaborative process—up to the point one disagrees enough to write a dissenting opinion. I believe you've heard my thinking on the amendment as of this moment, but listening to the other justices, assuming I'm confirmed, might or might not change what I think today."

"Are you good at standing up for yourself, Randolph?"

"Isn't that one of the reasons you nominated me, Madam President? My independence?"

♠

Randolph Cavendish left his second meeting with the President of the United States and waited in the stenographer's office for his copy of the conversation. He prided himself on getting in his point about 'independence,' but he understood—and worried—that Gloria Addison placed a different connotation on that word than him. Still, Cavendish thought it of some value the two did not appear at odds on the issue of guns in America. Indeed, he had been pleasantly surprised at her grasp of the central thrust of, and arguments vis-à-vis, the Second Amendment.

♠

President Addison had nominated Randolph Cavendish to the Supreme Court without a significant 'paper trail' of opinions that might elevate or sink him in the calculus of fence-sitting senators. People expected him to be a conservative justice, but that wasn't what lay behind his selection. No, his nomination was little more than Addison's hunch about the judge and the Second Amendment.

Cavendish was a 'stealth judge' whose professional record in the state courts and his short stint on the appeals court provoked little real controversy and provided that minimal 'paper trail' on issues of U.S. Constitutional law. One can only imagine Addison rubbing her hands together in satisfaction.

In testimony before the Senate, conservatives thought Cavendish a strict constructionist on constitutional matters with a keen interest in moderation.

"Our decisions will affect some human being for good or ill," he told the senators during the hearings on his nomination. "We'd better get it right."

In the state attorney general's office and as a state Supreme Court judge, neither position tested him on matters of federal law. Oddly, not a single senator asked him about the Second. They seemed obsessively concerned, however, with his view of *Roe v. Wade*. Would he vote to overturn? He parried each thrust from senators with repetitious statements, sometimes unctuous, of his dislike of radical change. He would attach high importance to precedent, he promised.

Some senators grumbled off stage that perhaps 'the nominee doth promise too much.'

EIGHTEEN

"You wanted to see me, General?"

Sean McKinnon was just being deferential. He knew exactly why the secretary had asked him to spend a few minutes of his time in the massive structure no one could possibly mistake as anything other than the Justice Department.

"Yes, Sean. Have a seat, please. Can I get you something? Coffee? Tea?"

McKinnon noticed that Jordan had his own coffee nook with a tray of fresh pastry.

"Yes, thanks, General. A coffee, please … And is that a chocolate croissant I see on that tray."

The attorney general's face lit up.

"You, too, huh, Sean. My favorite as well," he said as he approached the nook.

While the attorney general of the United States played waiter, McKinnon looked around the room. It seemed unusually large for one man. Several items on the walls stood out—a collage of photos of Jordan and other pols from his career, including Army buddies, and a large replica of Jordan's CIB (Combat Infantry Badge) from Vietnam. Sean had always heard that its recipients treasured that badge more than any medals for heroism.

But another item brought him near to tearing as he thought back to an earlier generation of idealists in this room trying to make the Republic live up to its promises. It was a photograph of Bobby Kennedy at his desk—the same, it appeared, that Jordan used—talking playfully with his small daughter Kerry.

McKinnon remembered a film he had seen of John Kennedy's struggle with a stubborn Governor George Wallace of Alabama as the President worriedly carried out a court order to integrate—desegregate—the University of Alabama. He remembered the distant, haunted look on the President face a few months before his assassination, as advisors inched him toward a decision to use the National Guard to enforce, if necessary, the court order. The President seemed to know the southern vote was slipping away. The photo of Bobby and his daughter appeared to be a frame from that film.

Jordan returned with the coffee and pastry, then pressed the button on his intercom. Sean McKinnon struggled to regain his composure.

"Nancy," Jordan said when she'd come into the room and seated herself, "see if the Director is on his way. If not, give him a jingle and remind him it's about our meeting with Sean McKinnon. He'll know the agenda."

"Right away," Nancy Drummond cooed in a manner so foreign to his ear it stopped Sean McKinnon from thinking whatever it was he was thinking.

♠

Jordan's executive assistant was a very attractive single woman who had come to D.C. right out of college, filled with the expectation—a solemn promise based on the experiences of the thousands who had preceded her—that Washington owed her a rewarding job and a husband. That she believed unreservedly. But the competition for jobs and men was fierce. So, Nancy's expectations and Washington's promise gradually lost their luster, morphing instead into a series of liaisons with husbands, true enough, but none of them hers.

The halls of the Justice Department, an enormous building with plenty of halls to echo rumors, was rife with the certainty only the water coolers and coffee nooks could confirm. Nancy had her sights on the biggest catch of all: the attorney general himself. First, though, she'd have to wrest him from his wife. Up and down the corridors of justice the betting was about even in Simon Jordan's pliancy to Nancy Drummond's machinations and, on the other hand, her adroitness.

♠

"Sean, I wanted to touch base with you before the Director and I go to the president with what could be a pretty serious threat to the country …"

The intercom buzzed.

"Yes, Nancy?"

She stood at the open door.

"The Director is here, sir."

The Director, *the* prima donna of prima donnas, insisted people only address or refer to him with a capital 'D.'

"Fine. Send him in."

"Sean, have you met Director Manning?"

"I haven't had the pleasure, but I've looked forward to it since we arrived in Washington."

Like all recent FBI directors, Matthew Manning began his ten-year-tenure under one president and would finish under another.

"It's a pleasure, Director," McKinnon said as they shook hands.

"Mine as well," Manning replied. "I hope you will give the President my regards."

"Of course."

McKinnon hesitated, not sure how the Director would receive what he was about to say; Sean was not a man of pretense. But, he decided, nothing ventured, nothing gained.

"Director, may I call you Matt?"

"'Matthew' will do, Mr. McKinnon, although I prefer 'Director Manning.' My mother was a big fan of the New Testament. She would expect that people honor her memory by respecting the name she gave her son. So, it's 'Matthew,' if you don't mind."

Jordan took a deep breath. McKinnon had his answer. Now he knew the rules of the game.

"Okay, gents, now that we've finished the introductions, let's discuss the reason we're here. Director?"

Manning didn't hesitate.

"How much do you know about militias, Mr. McKinnon?"

♠

NINETEEN

The Director's question alarmed McKinnon. He immediately sized up Manning as a direct, no-nonsense guy. He wondered if the President knew. She hadn't had much time to consider the character or other qualities of non-political actors like the Director. He suspected the Director had aimed his question as a probing action to learn what the President's knew. He was no longer the only White House person attendant.

"Not a lot," he replied honestly. "I've heard or read that Michigan has many militia groups. I suppose other states as well."

"Well, what we know exceeds Michigan exponentially. These are private organizations that include paramilitary or similar elements. They go by several names: militia, unorganized militia, and constitutional militia. The terms refer mostly to right-wing groups. By the mid-1990s, after earlier standoffs—our 1992 shootout with Weaver at Ruby Ridge and the 1993 Waco siege involving Koresh and the Branch Davidians—these groups were active in every state. We estimate there are between 10,000 and 250,000 of them."

Manning noticed that McKinnon had been taking notes.

"Should I slow down," he asked the chief of staff.

"No, no, I'm good. I just want to be able to recall the most significant of your points for the President."

"Got it. These militias claim that the law sanctions them, but the government cannot regulate them. They are purposed, they insist, to oppose a tyrannical government. The movement's ideology has led some adherents to commit criminal acts, including stockpiling illegal weapons and explosives …"

"Whoa! Hang on a second," McKinnon requested. "Considering the extensive reach of the Second Amendment, what weapons and explosives are illegal?"

"Give me a second to jog my memory and check my notes."

McKinnon nodded.

"Okay, I'll try to simplify. Illegal weapons include machine guns (sometimes called assault weapons capable of fully automatic, semiautomatic, or burst fire at the user's option, and any semiautomatic pistol that accepts a detachable magazine); sawed-off shot guns; explosives and bombs (dynamite, C-4, grenades); stilettos, switchblades, et cetera. We're not as worried about the knives as we are the rest."

Uncomfortable laughter.

"Some militias subscribe to the 'insurrection theory,' which lays out the right of the people to rebel against the established government in the face of tyranny. They generally share a common belief in the imminent or actual rise of a tyrannical government, which, they believe, they must confront through armed force. But they are wrong about the validity of the 'insurrection theory.' In 1951 the U.S. Supreme Court said that so long as the government guaranteed free elections and trials by jury, armed rebellion was prohibited."

"So, Sean," Jordan picked up, "you've heard about militias and illegal weapons. Now comes the difficult part and the principal reason I asked you here this morning …

"The Bureau has undercover agents in some of the militias, and they are reporting that something big is about to break. What it might be they haven't yet confirmed. Apparently, the militia leaders are keeping it need to know. So, we must be prepared for many things, including an assassination attempt on the President."

"What's behind all this?"

"Take a guess."

McKinnon looked at both men and thought for a moment before speaking.

"The Second?"

"Bingo! The number of mass shootings has riled up the gun safety people and some in Congress. That's got the NRA and its fellow travelers convinced the President is coming for their guns. Our undercover agents report an exponential increase in militia messaging, gun purchases, and quiet movement around the country."

"So, what can the Bureau do? How imminent is the coup you describe?"

"We estimate its only weeks away. Unfortunately, there's nothing direct the Bureau can do until there's an overt act. But we can warn the president and the Secret Service—that's why you're here—and put all levels of law enforcement on alert. But we must be subtle about that alert, ready for anything without giving away that we're on to them."

"You're baiting them into an attack of some kind? Seems to me that could backfire. They find a way to carry out their plan before you can react."

"Always a risk in law enforcement. We do have constitutional guarantees. Not to harp on the same point, but we need to be ready."

"Do you think their plan might be to assassinate leaders in all branches—to decapitate the government?"

"We think that's a stretch, Mr. McKinnon. Your job is as I said a moment ago, to inform the president and the Secret Service."

"She's still going to want to talk to you both about this—in person. And she'll demand hard evidence. I hope you have some."

"Of course," Jordan said as he stood, signaling an end to the meeting, "don't worry about that. Just get the ball rolling. We'll take it from there."

McKinnon thought he saw the same look on Jordan's face as that worn by Kennedy back in June 1963. He knew he'd have to shake off that memory if he were to do his job. How would he break the news he'd just heard to the President?

"Pleasure meeting you, Director," McKinnon lied as they headed toward the door."

"Yes, likewise," the Bureau chief responded. "My regards to the president. I'm always ready to serve."

"Goodbye, Mr. McKinnon," Nancy said as Sean passed near her desk. The way she said it made him a little uncomfortable. He didn't know why.

"Yes … Thank you, Ms. Drummond."

TWENTY

"Stephanie, see if the majority leader is free for a few minutes with his president, will you, please?"

"Of course, Ma'am.

"Three minutes later.

"Senator Clark on one, Ma'am."

"Phil, how're Martha and the kids?"

"They're all fine, Madam President. How can I help you?"

"What're we doing about this Second Amendment stuff? You got enough support to get some of those minor changes we've been discussing over the hump so I have something to sign, and we can save some lives?"

"I've got forty-seven to forty-eight certain …"

"Damn, senator! That's not going to cut it. I'm sure you know that. You can't even get to fifty?"

"Not yet. Those two or three senators represent states we didn't win, and those senators are petrified of their voters' wrath if they go for the minor gun safety bills that passed the House."

"Any pressure I can apply through executive authority? Favorite projects I can influence one way or the other? Emergency disaster funding? Not visiting their state?"

Senator Clark nearly gagged aloud over that one. These were not states where President Addison would be welcome.

"Right now, they're not going to budge, Madam President, unless the House bills undergo serious modification."

"You mean watered down to where they have no teeth."

"Yes, Ma'am."

"Should I invite them down here for a little arm twisting? I've got a good handle on the Second now. Maybe a little logic applied in small doses?"

"Worth a try, Ma'am."

"Thanks, Phil. Keep at it up there, okay. It's too important to give up this soon. Stay in touch."

"Yes, Ma'am."

She hung up the phone and turned to her chief of staff. You got any dirt we can use on that Wyoming SOB to get him off his duff? Same for Senator … F**k! Can't even think of the guy from South Dakota."

It always shocked Sean McKinnon to hear a woman use that word, especially someone from Cummins where no one, men included, ever used it.

"Brook, Ma'am. Senator Stephen Brook, the senior senator from South Dakota."

"Hmm. You suppose he's part Lakota? If not, maybe he's been screwing those tribes out there. Or helping them with a little under the table money for favorable Casino legislation? He's gotta be crooked, right? How many terms?

"He's been in Congress for nearly forty years."

"So, how does a guy get that kind of permanency without greasing some squeaky wheels here and there? Must be dirty hands all over those two states, reaching out for whatever they can get from Uncle. Can you get me a list of the pork Brook's pulled out of the budget over those forty years? Same for the senior senator from Wyoming whose name I do know: Hiram Westfield. I'm seriously considering having them down here one at a time for a little chat."

"I'll get the Budget Office to pull up the information you want, but we should look at it carefully … make sure we're on solid ground before we confront them. They've been around the block a few times, and you can be sure they'll have anticipated your move and your motive."

Incredulous at what she'd just heard, she glowered at him with deliberate menace, something he'd rarely seen her do, and he knew right away he'd stepped over a line. Gloria Addison wasn't a person, let alone the President of the United States, that one—especially her chief of staff—should have considered a rube, someone in need of instruction when it came to negotiations. She'd had plenty of practice at Cummins, and she'd thoroughly worked over the other aspirants for the job of president.

She finally broke the awkward silence. What she said may have sounded like a question, but it was an ill-disguised threat.

"You've got faith in me, don't you, Sean."

He understood it wasn't a question.

"Of course, Madam President."

But maybe the president's look, and her supposed question revealed a little *too* much hubris, too *much* cockiness, an all-too-common shortcoming of the powerful.

TWENTY-ONE

The president's individual tête-à-tête with Senators Brook and Westfield did not go as she had hoped. Sean's search through budget records unearthed nothing the president could use to pry a couple of votes out of either senator on what amounted to incremental steps at gun safety.

Each senator emerged from the White House to face reporters and a bank of microphones waiting in the driveway near the north portico. Once the hungry mob had quieted, each senator, in his own way, proceeded to mouth the kind of platitudes no reporter could possibly accept as satisfactory about a meeting that had accomplished nothing on the president's agenda.

One thing had occurred, and of that, naturally, neither senator said anything. But each had come to believe that the President of the United States was both an enemy of them personally and a mortal enemy of the constitutional rights of the people. She intended, they were positive, to take away their guns.

The two senators thought little of the reporters facing them, pathetic losers, they believed, jostling for attention, shouting superficial questions that did nothing to distract the lawmakers' from thinking about how to go after the president and defend their honor. Those assumptions about reporters, their own behavior in response to questions they didn't quite hear or understand, were, without exaggerating the point, how each had survived forty-plus years in cutthroat Washington. It was also the mindset of a gun-slinging Old West.

♠

"Ellen!" Senator Hiram Westfield bellowed as he stormed into his office, one of fifty in the Senate Hart Office Building. He tossed his hat in the direction of a clothes rack but missed.

"Shit!"

He slammed down his briefcase, not missing his desk as he had with his hat and the clothes rack. He was about to ask his executive assistant to place a call, an ill-advised request from a man rattled ever since he left the farcical press conference in the White House driveway, and ill-advised for another reason. What Hiram Westfield needed was a 'burner.'

"Yes, sir?" Ellen Bond replied.

"Never mind. Just cancel my remaining appointments, will you?"

"Including the Boy Scouts from Riverton?"

"Yeah, but make sure the Scouts get accommodations somewhere nice overnight. Take it out of my travel allotment. I'll see them tomorrow."

"Yes, sir. Can I get you anything? Aspirin? Tylenol? A Xanax? Some green tea?"

"No, thank you, Ellen. That's very sweet of you. Just make sure I'm not bothered for the next couple of hours … Oh, how did you know about the Xanax?"

"Senator! Really? I've been at your elbow for many years."

But he was no longer listening.

She thought the cancellations a strange development but went along and closed the door between their offices.

He approached a bookcase located between two windows, pulled out two books by William F. Buckley, and reached in. When he pulled back his hand it held a 'burner.' By that time, it was late in a Washington day, although still early in Lusk, Wyoming. Hiram Westfield was dead tired, physically and emotionally, and he promptly fell asleep on a couch still clutching the phone.

An hour later, before she left for the night, Ellen gently opened the door, saw it was dark, recognized her boss's snore, and quietly closed it. She knew such behavior from an octogenarian wasn't unusual, so she headed for the Beltway and her home in Reston, Virginia.

♠

Hiram Westfield slept until early the next morning. When he woke, nearly falling off the couch in the process, he noticed the 'burner' had slipped from his hand onto the floor. Then, he remembered what he needed it for, sat up, checked the time—6:45—and punched in a number he found in the crumpled notebook protruding from the back pocket of his trousers.

After a dozen or more rings, he heard the familiar unpleasant voice of a man he had chosen to call rather than others because of his obscurity.

"Goddammit, this had better be good! You got any idea what time it is?"

♠

TWENTY-TWO

Seventy-two days after his nomination a bipartisan Senate confirmed Judge Randolph Cavendish's nomination to a seat on the Supreme Court. As in all Senate legislation, except for carve-outs, successful passage of legislation and its 'advise and consent' role required the lawmakers to overcome a potential filibuster.

In the end, it worked as President Addison hoped. Cavendish won confirmation, but only by a whisker. The Senate Judiciary Committee had reported him out nine to eight. On the floor, sixty-one senators voted to confirm, thirty-five voted 'nay,' and four recorded themselves as 'present.' The Court had a new associate justice—by a whisker. But would the president have the justice she wanted and needed?

♠

Within the Court, discussions and opinion sharing about the Columbia, Missouri, assault weapons ban began in earnest. Justice Cavendish stuck to the playbook, which he considered an ultimatum—a contract of sorts—established during his conversations with the president. He stuck to her expectation until he couldn't. The ambiguity of the Second Amendment allowed the majority to take the route paved by Mateo Ricci. The 'operative' clause was an unambiguous expression of the individual right to 'keep and bear' firearms. There was more.

During their collaborative consideration of the Missouri law, the Chief Justice, Clarence Smallwood, invited Randolph to his private suite for lunch. They sat down to a Shrimp Louie, much admired by Cavendish, and a Chardonnay from Lohr. For dessert, the Chief's waitress served each a chocolate mousse.

They had made small talk as they dined—the weather, the overseas news of the day—the Chief trying to find a way to soften the blow he was about to deliver. Finally, the host placed his napkin on the table and sat back in his chair.

"I admire your devotion to the militia clause,"—he refused to call it the 'subordinate clause'—"Randolph and I agree it was the Founders' intent that possession of arms required militia service. But that hasn't been the Court's position historically, and now the country is swimming in weapons. There are more guns than people, if you can imagine."

Cavendish had already begun to see the direction of the Chief's argument. He wondered if he ought not excuse himself but realized that sort of protest wouldn't change anything, but it would be exceedingly rude and end any chance of his being an effective member of the Court in future cases. An image of the President's face quickly crossed his mind and disappeared just as fast. It was not a good look.

"If one were to respect the entirety of the amendment," Smallwood continued, "it would mean dispossessing—seizing—the weapons of millions of Americans who do not belong to a state militia, and that would have the additional problem of running afoul of due process guarantees. The result would certainly be revolution. So, this Court must never view the amendment in any other way than *Hendricks*. Don't you agree? The country cannot live with the Columbia, Missouri, ban."

While he contemplated what the Chief had just said and tried to formulate a reply, the Chief's undeniable logic reemphasized for Justice Randolph Cavendish the injustice of the 21st century rendering the 18th obsolete. Of course, any such idea about the relevance of the 18th century was not unfamiliar to many Americans, but Smallwood's view of the Second Amendment's suicidal potential ended any thought of rewriting the Constitution to satisfy critics who believed the document hopelessly outdated.

"Well, Justice Cavendish, what say you? And be candid, please. I tell every new justice that candor is the only way the Court can reach consensus, one way or the other …

"Oh, and one more thing. I wonder if in any manner the President instructed your position."

"I'll answer your second question first, because the other is so difficult. I can say two things about the President. One, she has strong views on the Second, and they don't align with *Hendricks*. Two, I believe she knew better than attempt to instruct me on how I might rule. She did share her views with me, and I also had an extensive discussion of the amendment with her chief of staff in which I briefed him in detail about the philosophical underpinnings of the amendment's two clauses ...

"Your argument about the practicality of *Hendricks* was both persuasive and frightening. I can't say more than that now, but I fear I could never mount a serious objection to your persuasive powers, although I might try desperately to do so. Your practical rather than judicial answer to overturning *Hendricks*, if revealed publicly, might well result in impeachment for any justice found to have subscribed to it."

"Thank you for *your* candor, Randolph. I can't say that I disagree with your logic should my explanation of why we must learn to live with *Hendricks* leak to the public."

♠

Six months later, in the last week of its term, the Supreme Court, by a vote of six to three, Justice Randolph Cavendish writing for the majority, found the Columbia, Missouri, ban on assault weapons unconstitutional.

At the White House it was as if someone had triggered a nuclear explosion.

♠

TWENTY-THREE

The scene in the Oval Office following the announcement of the *Columbia* decision defied a storyteller's imagination. Minutes … seconds after she learned of the Court's action, the President of the United States went ballistic. Sean McKinnon tried every technique he knew to calm his boss. He tried to hold back the added blow that Justice Cavendish had authored the majority opinion, but she heard about that anyway, shortly after the initial blow. She laced the next few minutes with profanity.

"That SOB betrayed me!" she screamed, only she didn't use the acronym. "That pissant from that pissant state! He sat right there," she pointed to the divan, "right there in that seat, and lied to my face—twice. Goddammit, Sean! I could kill the SOB! Everyone told me he was independent-minded. Well, someone got to him. The NRA? The other party? Did you see a weak point in him they might have used the squeeze him? Is he gay, maybe?"

"We vetted him thoroughly, so, I doubt he's gay, and I didn't detect any weaknesses during the vetting. He left me with the same impression as he did you, Madam President, independent-minded ... Come to think of it, that may be what we're looking for. Just to prove his independence to God-knows-who, maybe himself, he wasn't going to pay any attention to our opinions on the Second. That was the weakness … his insecurity."

"That's why the Chief assigned him the majority opinion! Buck him up. Make him feel like a big man."

"We've got to find a way to cut him down to size without taking him to the woodshed, so to speak. You sure there's no pressure point? Who are his friends? His best friend?"

"On his vetting form he listed one reference that might be worth looking into."

"Oh, yeah? Who?"

"A big corporate lawyer in Houston. Ralph Donaldson. I could make some discreet inquiries through contacts I had there when we were with Cummins."

"What kind of inquiries?"

"Whether he cut corners, legally or otherwise. Threaten exposure."

"You mean blackmail, *if* you find anything."

"Yes, I suppose I do.

"I have another idea. Find someone to make unpleasant things happen to Cavendish."

McKinnon looked at his boss, trying to measure her expression for the strength of her commitment to a plan of harassment. He knew she could be ruthless, of course, but this was a question involving the separation of powers between the branches. If anyone caught the White House attempting to corrupt another branch of government, it would surely bring in the Justice Department, and Simon Jordan might be itching to do just that.

"How 'unpleasant' were you thinking?" Sean asked, breaking his thoughtful silence. "I might know a guy. But you'd also need to keep the Justice Department at bay. Do you believe the guy you defeated for the nomination would go for that?"

"Good question. There's a third possibility. Pressure Congress to pass some sane gun safety legislation."

"That will take public pressure and time. Meanwhile, the slaughter will continue. Madam President, I hate to say this, but the only way to get Congress to take the issue seriously will be when they or their kids are the targets."

"I thought only I had thoughts like that."

"Well, I'd bet you and I are not alone. Seems logical."

"It's not gonna happen, Sean. So, I'm back to Cavendish? Where we started."

"I'll touch bases with my guy in Houston, see what might turn up there."

"Okay, what's next …"

TWENTY-FOUR

Clinton Downey wasn't what one might call introspective. He seemed incapable of understanding rejection, a regular visitor at his door. Nonetheless, he tried one morning to take took stock of his life, the first time he'd done so since his divorce months earlier. It wasn't clear what made that morning special. Perhaps he just slept better. Perhaps it was last night's supper. Still, it happened, which was beside the point.

He'd lost an election to a woman and was divorced by another. But those setbacks only temporarily took his mind away from a grandiose goal, the one he took stock of that morning, the one that would restore his sense of self and return the United States to a constitutional government.

Downey's thinking wasn't unique. The reason for his and other's setbacks always, they insisted, lay outside themselves, never within. Those shapeless, outside forces deliberately acted to persecute and foil any chance those like Downey might have for success. Only the lone actor who had suffered setback after setback at the hands of the power elite had the vision to understand the true reason for his inability to advance and the willingness to sacrifice himself to set things straight.

Clinton Downey knew that setting things straight would not be pretty. Those undefined outside forces would never voluntarily relinquish their hold over him. The only power he believed he could wield to restore constitutional government was to stop efforts in Washington and elsewhere from overturning or skirting the Second Amendment. Clifford Downey's power was the power of the gun. Without the Second, he would be helpless, stripped not only of self-esteem but a future.

Downey wasn't a religious man, but at the Sunday School his mother forced him to attend he'd absorbed enough of the Old Testament to persuade him of the commonsense truth of 'an eye for an eye.' His mother's church, however, wasn't much into the New Testament, the 'Golden Rule' and so much more. It sounded ideal, but it defied human nature and common sense, as Downey saw it.

So, he'd awakened that morning believing the responsibility of preventing further erosion of the Second Amendment belonged to him. Attacking the source of the problem in Washington would make Clinton Downey and the country whole. Then maybe, just maybe, women would pay attention to him.

♠

He waited until nine o'clock and then placed a call to an acquaintance in the insurance business in another state and a member of the NRA. Downey figured that man knew someone who knew someone who, he surmised, might have access to at least one of the elected 76 NRA directors across the country.

"Clint! Long time; no see. Heard about your divorce. Sorry, man. *Que pasa*?"

Downey came straight to the point. Such was his agitation he might have sounded angry to the man at the other end, but he wasn't.

"Max, do you know what the NRA's doing about all this crap in Washington to grab our guns? Someone's got to stop it!"

'Max' was Maxwell Lewis of Nebraska.

"Clint, all I know is the NRA is doing what it always does, lobbies Congress and begs us for money."

Max stopped and thought for a moment.

"But look, depending how serious you are, you might consider joining a group that calls itself, I think, 'Sons of Freedom.' You'd have to get in shape. They do a lot of outdoor training. You'd need free time. Take orders. Real military-like stuff. You have weapons? Tactical gear?"

"Weapons? Yeah. No problem there. What's 'tactical gear'?"

"Vest. Helmet. Gear that will deflect or stop rounds. Belt to carry magazines."

"Okay, thanks for that. But I'm serious, Max, and I'm sure I could manage. Who are these guys?"

"It's a militia bunch that started in Montana."

"Damn, Montana's a long way from Indiana."

"I wouldn't worry about that. Militias from different states coordinate and operate jointly."

"'Sons of Freedom.' Sounds familiar."

"Yeah, I think they took that name from the 'Sons of Liberty,' that bunch during the Revolution. Look, why don't you go to your library and do some research?"

"Great idea, thanks!"

♠

Downey wasn't sure a militia was right for him. He could never be sure, he thought, that their goals and his matched. But he decided to find a library and educate himself about the Sons of Liberty and militias in general:

> The **Sons of Liberty** was a grassroots group of instigators and provocateurs in colonial America who used an extreme form of civil disobedience—threats, and in some cases actual violence—to intimidate loyalists and outrage the British government.
>
> The Sons likely formed from a secretive group of nine Boston-based patriots who called themselves the Loyal Nine. The first Sons chapters sprung up in Boston and New York City, but other cells soon appeared in other colonies as well.
>
> The group may have taken its name from a speech given in Parliament by Isaac Barre, an Irish member sympathetic to the colonists, who warned that the British

government's behavior "has caused the blood of these sons of liberty to recoil within them."

The Sons' most prominent leader was Sam Adams, the son of a wealthy brewer who was more interested in radical rabble-rousing than commerce.

Another key member was John Hancock, later immortalized by his flamboyant signature on the Declaration of Independence. James Otis, Paul Revere, Benedict Arnold, and Dr. Benjamin Rush were also involved.

The Sons' defiance of the British helped spur the Revolutionary War and fostered an American tradition of grassroots activism that various activist groups have adopted to push for change.

He decided if the 'Sons of Freedom' were anything like what he'd just read, he might change his mind. But he wasn't sure the 'Sons of Liberty' was a militia, so he kept looking until he found this:

A **militia** is generally an army or some other fighting organization of non-professional.

Militias can be military or paramilitary. They may be:

Forces engaged to protect a community, its territory, property, and laws,

The entire able-bodied population of a community, town, county, or state.

A private (non-governmental) force.

An irregular armed force that enables its leader to exercise military, economic, or political control over territory within a sovereign state,

Colonial militias came from the body of adult male citizens.

In the colonial era a militia existed to meet a threat for a limited time. Militia members provided their own weapons and equipment.

In *Leavenworth, Washington v. Hendricks*, the Court made explicit in its *obiter dicta*, that the term 'militia,' as used in colonial times, included both the federally organized militia and citizen-organized militias.

Today, private militia organizations in the United States often have an anti-government outlook and are not under the civil authority of the states.

♠

"Max Lewis?" the voice at the other end said hesitantly.

"Yeah, who's this?"

"You on the right kind of phone, Max?"

"No, but let me grab one. Call me back in two minutes."

Four minutes later …

"Lewis?"

"Yeah, I'm secure now. *Que pasa*?"

"Look, Lewis, my name is Hank Lockwood. I got a call from a guy named Downey. He said you recommended our group. He might want to join. Is this guy legit?"

"Hank, call me Max, okay? I don't know what kind of member Clint would be. Right now, he's just a barrel full of anger about attempts on the Second. I've known him for several years. We're both in the insurance and associated businesses. Character-wise, I'd say okay. Not a very good salesman. Whether he's physically fit enough for the group, I can't say."

"Best guess, Max?"

"Marginal but try him. He'll take orders; that's for sure."

"You have any reason to think he might be working for the other side?"

"Absolutely not!"

"Okay, Max. Tell the guy to meet me at the Pizza Hut at 2508 Preston Highway in Louisville at 1400 on the 19th, and in future let me know before you circulate my name."

"Roger that, Hank. Sorry about the protocol screw-up."

Hank Lockwood rang off without saying goodbye.

Chagrined, Lewis pocketed his phone. He knew he'd screwed up, but there was nothing he could do about it.

'That's what you get for helping a friend,' he mused.

♠

Downey did not keep the appointment with Hank Lockwood, although Max Lewis had passed along the information about time and place.

The reason for his failure to follow through wasn't clear. Perhaps he didn't like the arrangements. Perhaps he was never that interested in a militia in the first place and was just exploring options with Lewis.

"Lewis?"

"Yeah?"

"That asshole you set me up with, the guy you said wanted to join a militia …"

Lewis cut him off.

"So, what about him?"

"What about him? *What about him?* He never showed! You sent me a guy who gave us every indication of working for the other side. Now he's got my name, and he knows where I meet people! Don't you ever bother calling me again … about anything!"

Hank Lockwood threw his phone at the wall, sending pieces flying in every direction.

Max Lewis decided he'd better junk his phone, which suddenly felt dirty, and get another.

♠

TWENTY-FIVE

Martha Breyer rang her boss, Ralph Donaldson.

"I know you're with clients, but I have a Mr. Powers on the line. This is the third time he's called. He'd still like a few minutes of your time before the end of the week. He won't say why, only that he works at the White House."

"Alright, goddammit! Put him down for Thursday, any time in the morning. He'll have to adjust *his* schedule if he wants some of my time."

The clients in Donaldson's office, a couple of oil lobbyists who wanted to hear the firm's position on pending lease legislation in Congress, looked at each other with semi-embarrassment and raised eyebrows.

"He'll see you Thursday at 11:10, Mr. Powers," Breyer informed the caller.

♠

"What'd you say your name was? And who gave you my name?"

Ben Powers had managed to get the appointment, despite Ralph Donaldson's initial stone-walling, but Powers was persuasive and stubborn. In addition to those personal characteristics, it didn't hurt his cause that he was an emissary from the White House.

"I didn't mention either," Sean McKinnon's investigator replied to Donaldson. "I'm Ben Powers and I'm here at the request of the president's chief of staff."

The busy Houston lawyer believed he needed to accede to a request from the White House. And he was curious what brought someone close to President Addison to Texas.

"In a nutshell, Mr. Donaldson, I want to know if you are willing help your country?"

"Bullshit!" Donaldson shouted. "What kind of bullshit question is that? You know goddamn well I always help my country, my president, when I can. For Chris' sakes!"

Unshaken, Ben Powers lied.

"Certain unsavory allegations about your old friend Justice Cavendish have reached the president. I'm here to make sure we can put those scurrilous attacks behind us."

Donaldson took in what he'd just heard, then leaned forward in his chair.

"So, Mr. Powers, if that's really who you are, let me get this straight. One, you're bluffing. No 'allegations' came to you. Two, it sounds like you people put my buddy on the Court, he ruled against you, and now you want me to give up something unseemly about his past so you can have him impeached or force him to retire. That about it? Where the f**k did you get the balls to come down here and ask me to do anything remotely like that?"

"Aren't you protesting a bit too much? Sounds like you do have something to tell me. If Justice Cavendish lied on his vetting form and lied to Congress, don't you think the American people have a right to know and the president a right to challenge the legitimacy of Cavendish's nomination and confirmation?"

Donaldson pressed a button on his phone console. When she appeared at the door, Donaldson spoke firmly. "Martha, please call security. Mr. Powers was just leaving."

"Don't you have some pending leases before Congress?" Powers said calmly, as though he were confident what affect his words would have.

Donaldson returned Powers's gaze.

"Hold off on security, Martha."

"Are you sure?"

"Yes, for now. Thank you, Martha."

"I see I jogged your memory, Mr. Donaldson."

"You people are real sonsabitches, you know that."

"When was the last time you spoke to your conscience," Mr. Donaldson? It sure didn't take much for me to get through to you about the seriousness of this situation. Just the slightest mention of your company's investment and you're ready to go all *quid pro quo*."

"I didn't say I'd cooperate with you, Powers."

"Oh, no? Then why did you call off security the instant I mentioned those leases?"

Donaldson leaned back in his chair. His eyes turned misty. Powers could tell the lawyer was deeply conflicted. Betrayal usually does that to a person.

"You're not leaving here without a written stipulation regarding those pending leases. Is that clear?"

"I'll decide the wording of that stipulation."

"And I'll need a signed statement that you did not get anything out of me of harm to my friend."

"Okay, I can do that."

Donaldson pondered his visitor for some sign Powers'd let him off the hook. Sean McKinnon's man gave none. So, he caved. Those leases were worth billions. Friends were without monetary value.

"Alright, then. There was a party, lots of us there, men and women—boys and girls, really. I think it was our junior year. Spring. You know how that is. It happened at a frat house, not ours. People got drunk. People found the dorm on the third floor and turned it into an orgy. Drunken guys screwing girls who passed out or were too drunk to say, 'no' …

"I think two or three of them wound up pregnant, and one of them named Randy. It was rape. All of it. Not just Randy. I'm not trying to sugarcoat what he did, what all of us did …

"Long story short, ol' man Cavendish arranged for an abortion. He wanted it to remain on the hush-hush. He got her to sign a non-disclosure agreement in return for his handling the abortion. You probably know that Randy switched undergraduate colleges, but you didn't know why until now."

"Wow!" was all Powers could say at that moment. Then, he gathered himself.

"I'll say this about you, Mr. Donaldson. When you go *quid pro quo*, you really go *quid pro quo*!"

"You didn't get this from me. Understood?"

"I'm sure I can arrange it that way, of course. But this is crucial; I'll need a date for that 'party.'"

"I'll get it. One of those things in life that never leaves you. Now," Donaldson bore in, "before you go back to the president with this, Mr. Powers, let's get down to business about those leases."

♠

"Jesus H. Christ, Sean! Can we back this up? We gotta be able to do that."

"Ben said he followed up with the doctor that Donaldson named, and he confirmed it in writing—notarized. He was reluctant at first—doctor/patient confidentiality—to give Ben any information. I reminded him of the stakes involved—a corrupt Supreme Court justice who should, at a minimum, face a perjury charge if the allegation of an abortion were true. That persuaded him to cooperate …

"He found the file without the help of any staff, by the way, and told me it showed that ol' man Cavendish arranged for the abortion a few months after the orgy; the dates lined up. The file included an affidavit from the girl that Cavendish was the father. We can say the doctor came to us to clear his conscience. That leaves Donaldson out of it."

"What if Congress subpoenas the doc?"

"He'll stand on doctor/patient confidentiality and take the Fifth, if necessary."

"And possibly go to jail—for us?" I'm leery of him doing that, I can tell you."

"We will deal with that possibility when it becomes necessary. We can always fall back on Cavendish's lawyer friend in Houston as the source. Bottom line: Cavendish betrayed you, Madam President."

"Jesus H. Christ," she muttered again. Mr. Goody-Two-Shoes Cavendish … shush."

TWENTY-SIX

President Addison faced a plethora of tough decisions on major issues and additional choices on subsidiary questions. She believed, not wrongly, that Justice Cavendish had betrayed her with his vote on the Columbia, Missouri, decision. She had evidence he withheld vital information, disqualifying information, during his vetting and confirmation hearings to guarantee his having a seat on the Court.

Initially, it made sense to the president to confer with representatives of the two other branches of government: the Chief Justice and the majority and minority leaders of the Senate. She intended in the first instance to learn what discipline, if any, the Court intended to impose, and in the second, to discuss the nominee's conduct during his Senate hearing; it appeared to President Addison that the nominee had subverted its Constitutional advice and consent role. The question that weighed most heavily on the president was how much of the rape/abortion evidence she must reveal to get either or both institutions to take action against Cavendish. Neither the chief justice nor the senators would do so without sufficient cause. She could rely on the doctor/patient confidentiality argument, of course, but only to a point. Then what?

"You'll just have to cross that bridge when you come to it," Sean McKinnon offered weakly, falling back on advice he frequently employed.

Addison looked at her chief of staff, as if to say, 'thanks for nothing.'

"Let's get Simon over here and figure out what, if any, legal roadblocks or opportunities there are for this conundrum."

"Okay, but in the meantime, I think you should start thinking about a replacement for Cavendish. I'll talk to Simon."

♠

"Thanks for coming, Simon. We've got a real shitstorm brewing. I don't know how much Sean told you, if anything …"

Jordan saw where she was going and cut her off.

"Nothing, Madam President, only that you needed some legal advice. I suppose that's what the 'shitstorm' is about?"

"Right. Okay, let's start with the Court's opinion on the Columbia, Missouri, case. You know, of course, that despite everything he told Sean and me, Cavendish actually … *he* wrote the majority opinion!"

"Yes, I am aware."

The president, red-faced, took some deep breaths.

"But here's what you don't know and where this thing gets sticky. Cavendish hid from everyone an important character flaw from his past. We have the evidence that while in college he raped a young woman at a frat party-turned-orgy. Both were drunk as skunks. Cavendish's father arranged for an abortion. Sean persuaded the doctor involved to let him see the file."

"He let you see a confidential file? He didn't squawk because of doctor/patient confidentiality?"

"Yeah, he squawked, but I can be very persuasive, especially when acting as an emissary of the president. I sold him on national security grounds and patriotism."

"How long is he gonna buy that? When reporters start calling and knocking? Then what? I'll tell you what. He's gonna spill the beans on the whole thing. He'll do that to keep his license and, just maybe, because he's a decent, honest guy."

"Wait, Simon, there's more. Sean found out about the rape/abortion from a lawyer pal of Cavendish's in Houston. That's where he got the doctor's name."

"Why would the lawyer do that?"

"Well, he squawked at first, too, but I arranged a *quid pro quo*."

"Must have been a doozy. What'd we give up?"

"Some oil leases stalled in Congress, which reminds me, Sean, in addition to discussing the Cavendish business with the leadership, we've got to give them a darn good reason to follow up with those leases. Make a note."

"Just when does that Houston lawyer expect to get those leases?" Jordan asked. "If he gets tired of waiting for Congress, which would be understandable, he could pull out of Sean's arrangement and blow this thing out of the water. Sean called it a *quid pro quo*, but I could easily foresee some intrepid journalist, whose been tracking the progress of those leases, making a call to Houston. Some people would call a *quid pro quo* a 'corrupt bargain. No offense, Sean. Just something to consider."

"Finished, Simon?"

"No, Madam President. May I speak frankly?"

"Go ahead."

"You asked me here for my advice, and I think there's more you need to consider."

"Yes?"

"The Houston lawyer might not repeat the rape/abortion part of the story to a reporter, but he might tell him or her that he did make a deal with the President of the United States. What kind of deal, the reporter wants to know? Then, we're off to the races. The media begins to run wild with speculation. Your opponents in Congress insist on hearings, and so forth ...

"At that point, you might begin to hear the word 'impeach.'" The President of the United States went looking for a sordid situation. But it turned out to be the sort of situation that was nothing new under the sun. She did this as an excuse to replace a justice who decided against her point of view. I'm sure you're aware that whatever the Court decides pisses off someone. I think you might be on the verge of dangerously overreaching, Madam President."

Gloria Addison stared blankly ahead, almost as though she were in a trance. Jordan noticed it and decided to tack in another direction.

"Madam President, if you might allow me to offer some advice …"

"Haven't you already? That's what you presumed to do as soon as you walked through the door."

The attorney general decided to ignore her sarcasm and her accusation. He threw her a curve and she whiffed. He was beginning to feel sympathy for her for the first time since their bitter nomination battle.

"Get out ahead of the story," Jordan began. "Go to the Chief with it. Don't tell him where you got it, but … Do you have some document to show him? Something that doesn't implicate the lawyer or the doctor? Wasn't there a court adjudication of the rape business?"

President Addison shrugged and looked at McKinnon, who nodded. Addison didn't know what his nod meant.

"Urge the Chief to get Cavendish to retire. Let him show the justice your document. Tell him some reporters are looking into it. He's clever enough to know what happens next. Have the Chief suggest he could plead ill health."

"What do you think, Sean?" she asked.

"I'll have one of my investigators look for any adjudication of the rape charges."

The president rose, followed by the two men.

"Appreciate your coming over on short notice, Simon … and the advice. I'll keep you apprised of things as they develop."

"One last suggestion, Madam President, if you will permit me."

"Why stop now, Simon."

More sarcasm to ignore, he thought.

"Why not forget the who thing … getting rid of Cavendish? Are you doing it solely because you're peeved at him over the gun ban decision?"

"As I said, Simon, I'll keep you in the loop as things develop."

They shook hands, leaving McKinnon alone with the president.

"You see that, Sean? Folded like a cheap suit. Not strong. That's why I beat him."

McKinnon smiled and nodded, wordlessly.

♠

TWENTY-SEVEN

Randolph Cavendish walked into the Chief Justice's chambers nine days after Jordan cautioned the president about going after the new justice.

"Good morning, sir."

"Have a seat, Mr. Justice Cavendish. May I call you Randolph?"

"Please, Mr. Chief Justice."

"Let's forget the formalities, shall we, Randolph?"

The directive rolled off the Chief's tongue with a bit of an edge. It wasn't so much a friendly, informal gesture as it was one that smacked of, 'Let's cut the crap, shall we?'

"Yes, sir," Cavendish replied, trying to sound as though he took the Chief's words as friendly and informal. But Cavendish had been around the block, and he knew what was coming.

"Marjorie?" the Chief called into the adjoining room. Cavendish had left the door open when he came in.

"Yes, sir?"

The Chief turned back to his guest.

"Brandy, Randolph? Or is it too early for you?"

"Just some tea, please."

"Right."

The Chief now had confirmation of a tight ass for a colleague.

"One special and one tea, Marjorie."

When she returned with the refreshments, the Chief asked her to close the door.

♠

Clarence Smallwood, Chief Justice of the Supreme Court, had been so for nearly twenty years. Smallwood was one of those southerners, a North Carolinian, who took a dim view of those from the deep South, Alabamians, Mississippians, Louisianians, the cotton and crayfish crowd he derisively called them. Nor did he think much of Yankees and, frankly, didn't think there was anything at all to brag about west of the Mississippi. He was a coastal Carolina and Duke Law School southerner and figured there wasn't much else to care about except to maintain the pretense of that birthright. Pretense was everything in the life of Clarence Smallwood.

So, he now had a justice on his hands who, if he had any pretense, as Smallwood thought he should, it had collapsed. Today, he had a handful of nasty business that needed closure. Central to that nastiness was a document presented to him by the president's chief of staff. Smallwood needn't have been the sharpest lawyer on the Court, which he wasn't, to realize Sean McKinnon had handed him pure dynamite.

Before meeting with the 'teetotaler,' he read Sean's document over and over, trying to grasp how someone like Randolph Cavendish, who had committed the act the document clearly established, had managed to worm his way onto Smallwood's Court. But the Chief was all about pretense, and that meant going forward by pretending Justice Cavendish had simply ceased to exist.

"Randolph, I want you to look at this affidavit filed by the young woman in question."

Cavendish took the paper and began to read. Almost immediately he lowered it with one had to his lap.

"May I ask how you came by this?" Cavendish said, waving the paper in his hand.

"You may not! I just want to know if this is true, Randolph. I want an explanation for the assertion in this sworn affidavit. Some girl accused you of rape?"

"It was all made up, Mr. Chief Justice."

Cavendish wasn't feeling informal any longer.

"There was never any proof I attended the party where this allegedly took place. Mistaken identity. Simple."

"So, you knew she filed this affidavit!"

"Yes, of course I knew."

"And if it was 'mistaken identity' why did your father pay for her abortion?"

"I don't know anything about that! My father never told me he had done so. I have no idea why he might have, since it wasn't me who impregnated her. How do you know about this alleged abortion?"

"We have an affidavit from the doctor. Are there any other bombshells like this one out there?"

"Hell, I don't know. It was a long time ago. Who knows what bitter people will come up with to extort you!"

"Don't get snippy with me! Who extorted you? For how much?"

"That was just a figure of speech. I simply meant that people wanted me to be guilty of something I wasn't. My enemies sent you this document and that doctor perjured himself to get me off the Court."

"Mr. Justice Cavendish," the Chief, too, dropped the earlier informality, "the Court can't stand the scrutiny that will come of this. I have shown you one document, but you and I know where there's smoke there's fire. If they—your so-called enemies—have that," and he pointed to the paper still in Cavendish's hand, "they have more. I can't wait for that to happen. I have the authority of this Court to protect. It must have the respect of the American people …

"You have a fine record as a jurist, Mr. Justice, indeed an exemplary one. I'm sure neither of us wants to see it tarnished by this sort of scandal. I believe you have it within your power to prevent that happening."

Cavendish began to squirm in his chair. He knew what the Chief was about to say.

"Therefore, I want you to resign, Mr. Justice. You can announce that your health prevents you from functioning as you must. Make up some debilitating disease. Consult with your physician. He'll know what to propose."

"Respectfully, Mr. Chief Justice, I have no intention of doing what you ask. I will not retire because of some phony accusation about me when I was a college student."

"You *will* do it!" Clarence Smallwood sputtered. "I'm no longer asking you politely. If you don't announce your retirement from the Court within twenty-four hours, I shall!"

"Marjorie," he said in a high state of anxiety into the phone console on his desk, "Mr. Justice Cavendish was just leaving. Please show him out!"

♠

"The Chief Justice on two, Madam President," Stephanie Quach intoned into the intercom after her boss picked up the phone.

Addison put the phone on 'speaker.' She wanted her chief of staff to hear everything.

"Hello, Mr. Chief Justice. What news?"

"Madam President, I'm afraid the news is not good. Justice Cavendish was quite clear he has no intention of retiring. He was indignant about the claim against him in Mr. McKinnon's document and believes the doctor perjured himself. It's the work of his 'enemies' he claims, people who don't want him on the Court. But he couldn't give me a reason for their opposition to him."

Gloria Addison bit her lip and silently pounded the fat side of her fist on the *Resolute* desk. Sean McKinnon rose from his chair and moved toward the president.

"I played to his ego," Smallwood continued, "but he was having none of it. I gave him twenty-four hours to announce his retirement, or I'd do it for him."

Sean McKinnon looked at his boss and winced.

"We need more time to think this over, Mr. Chief Justice. Why don't you call him up or stop by his chambers. Tell him you've changed your mind. Give him a week."

"Yes, Madam President. Before I ring off, may I ask you something?"

"Why, yes. Of course."

"Has this something to do with his vote on the Columbia, Missouri, case?"

McKinnon winced again.

"I'm surprised you'd ask me such a question, Mr. Chief Justice. You must know I couldn't possibly answer it," the president said in the most indignant-sounding voice she could manage.

Addison had deftly managed neither a 'yes' nor a 'no' to the Chief's impertinent question.

"Thank you, Madam President. May I speak frankly?"

"Please."

"I am relieved to know your office would not stoop so low as to take retribution on a sitting justice of the United States Supreme Court for a carefully considered decision. It would do immense harm to the rule of law and the exercise of equal justice in our country were it even *suspected* that the executive was behind such a plot against a co-equal branch of the government. I'm sure it would appall the Founders, too, were they to find such an incursion even under consideration. I have always believed we must be true to their vision, one that has guided us for more than two hundred years. Have a pleasant afternoon, Madam President."

He rang off so quickly the president had no chance to respond, other than sputtering expletives.

In the outer office, Stephanie Quach, who didn't need to be proficient in the French language and was not unaccustomed to President Addison's explosive temper, heard the repetition of one word in her tirade: *Merde*!

♠

TWENTY-EIGHT

"Those sonsabitches up there at the Court have no idea how strongly I feel about this issue and how determined I am to make this country safer," Gloria Addison exploded to her chief of staff. "What did you think about the Chief Justice's position, Sean? Is he going to hold Cavendish to twenty-four hours or a week?"

"He didn't say, did he. My guess would be he wants to avoid a confrontation with Cavendish, so, he'll go for a week's hiatus."

McKinnon deliberately avoided the president's question about Smallwood's personal view, the one that had caused his boss's verbal explosion.

"Well, Sean?"

"Well, what, Madam President?"

"I'm waiting …"

"Honestly, Madam President, the Chief's sign off rather impressed me. I think for now you're stuck with Cavendish and the NRA. You're not going to get any satisfactory help from Congress until some gun nut or gun nuts show up on Capitol Hill and start killing congressmen …

"That's just it, isn't it? It hasn't come home to them as it has to their constituents and the children of their constituents. What's left of them may finally see where we're headed and do something about it."

McKinnon's reaction didn't please the president. No one had spoken to her about Congress like that.

'Why?' she wondered. 'It made so much sense considering how pusillanimous they were in the face of NRA threats.'

But she was exhausted that evening, tired of fighting everyone over the threat to the Republic posed by the Second Amendment.

"I'm going up to the residence where I can relax, Sean, so, why don't you go home early as well."

"You won't have to say it twice, Madam President. Should I tell Stephanie to go home on my way out?"

"Yes, thank you, Sean. And thanks for your honesty about the justices. I'm still processing it."

♠

The president asked her body woman to have someone on the residence staff draw a hot bath. Minutes later, as she slid as low in the water as she could while still able to breathe, much was on her mind. She let memories of the past in Columbus shove aside current politics until the water turned tepid and soapy.

♠

Young Gloria Addison, 'Glory' Addison to some in a teasing mood, belonged to a fortunate generation some have said. Hers was a generation, the first of the 20th century, to emerge forever—it seemed for a time, anyway—from the scourge either of economic depression or war. The 'silent generation' as it came to be known, suggested that Gloria and her mates would neither be dissatisfied nor revolutionary. She'd read it somewhere. Time had obliterated the source, but it was something that sticks with a person:

> *After the horrors of World War II, the Silent Generation would spend its early adulthood in the shadow of a devastated social order .... Unlike the previous generation who had fought for 'changing the system,' the Silent Generation were about 'working within the system.' They were not risk takers.*
>
> *Their childhood experiences during the Depression and the insistence of their parents that they be frugal taught them thrift ...*

It didn't hurt the 'Silents,' of course, that their parents made sure they would have a secure future. Columbus, Indiana, Gloria's hometown, drank deeply of that mood and prosperity: a thriving industry—Cummins—to satisfy bills and enhance bank accounts—with some left over for pleasure—and rich farmland all 'round.

Railroad tracks held many fond memories. She'd pack a lunch and fill a war surplus canteen with water, and just hike along the tracks as far as adventuring allowed that day. She loved how the rails glistened and shimmered in the hot summer sun.

♠

White-framed, porched, faux-Victorian houses that dominated Columbus. Porches were integral to the affairs of the community. From them on a warm summer afternoon or early evening one could spot housewives in their rocking chairs, fanning themselves and sipping lemonade or iced tea. Like lords of a domain, they greeted and chatted with passersby about politics, the economy, or the latest town gossip, which too often meant who is sleeping with whom and shouldn't be? Does so-and-so know?

♠

Gloria learned politics from her mother. Margaret Addison believed herself more politically independent than her husband, but that wasn't quite true. Independent? Perhaps. But never to the extent of voting for anyone of a certain party.

Margaret Addison enthusiastically took part in causes favored by the League of Women Voters. When the tenor of politicians or opinion writers offended Margaret, she would pen a 'Letter to the Editor,' disguising her sex by using only her first two initials and her married name: 'M.C. Addison.' Absent a shred of reliable evidence and with unshakable certainty, she trumpeted the view that no editor would ever publish a woman's opinion about anything. Gloria determined from a young age that should politics ever interest her beyond simply voting, she would do something to change those editors' minds.

♠

By now the bath water had cooled but not Gloria's belief in her betrayal by Justice Cavendish and the spineless Chief Justice. Thinking back to the simpler days of her youth had reminded her of another Columbus name—David Charles, a classmate, who knew someone who knew someone who knew a guy ...

♠

TWENTY-NINE

"Madame President! Gloria! This *is* a surprise … and a pleasure," he hastened to add while covering the microphone on his cell phone.

"Honey! You'll never guess who's on the phone."

"Let me guess. Gloria Addison. It was a dead giveaway, Dave, when you shouted her name," she chided, laughing.

"Shit," he muttered.

"What's the occasion, Gloria? Are you resigning and coming home?" he said, somewhere between sarcasm and hope.

"Dave, shut-up and listen. Do you have a special phone?"

"You're asking me that because I'm a lawyer with shady clients? Where's the trust, girl?"

"Dammit, Dave. Shut-up and call me back on that phone. You're breaking up on this one."

Dave Charles was clever enough to know that when the president called, which she rarely did, it had to do with her need for confidentiality. He got out his throwaway, only two days old, looked at the number in his recent list on the first phone and dialed the President of the United States, his prom date their junior year.

"May I call you Gloria, or are we sticking to protocol?"

"Much as I'd like to dispense with formalities, I think it should be Madam President."

"Roger that."

Dave Charles had spent six years in the Navy as an F-4 Phantom RIO (radar intercept officer), resigning as a lieutenant. Then it was on to law school at Indiana University. It had never been clear to anyone why or how Dave became involved with people on the shady side of the law, but for some reason he felt more comfortable with their lack of pretense. Maybe there was a piece of Dave that craved danger, thumbing his nose at danger as though it could never touch him, just as he had in the Navy.

"Look, Dave, I've got a problem that requires the talent of that special someone."

He hadn't expected that one. He spent a few moments in thought, letting the word 'special' sink in. Suddenly, he didn't like the direction of their conversation.

"How special?"

"As special as it gets."

"Jesus H. Christ! Gloria," he exploded.

"Remember who you're talking to, Dave. I'm not your prom date any longer. Settle down and strap in. This isn't a drill, sailor!"

"I didn't think you were Gloria Addison, sweet sixteen and the belle of the ball, Madam President, but you asked me for a favor. If you truly want my help, I deserve *your* respect. Otherwise, it's been nice talking to you."

"Okay, okay, Lieutenant. I apologize … I asked for this job, but it feels like the whole world is crashing down on me. I didn't intend to take it out on you, so, let's start over. Shall we?"

"Sure. We were at 'as special as they get.'"

"You ever see *Apocalypse Now*?"

"Sure. Why?"

"There's a line in the film when a superior officer briefs Martin Sheen on his mission to find Colonel Kurtz—Marlon Brando. The officer tells Sheen to terminate the colonel's command. Naturally, Sheen is confused about such a vague order, and he asks, 'Terminate the Colonel?' Then, a civilian in the room puts a fine point on the order: 'terminate with extreme prejudice.'

She paused to let him grasp why she had called.

"You remember that?"

"I had hoped you weren't going there, Madam President. Are you?"

"The SOB betrayed me, Dave! He sat right here in the Oval and lied. He lied to the Senate during his confirmation. Then, he lied to the Chief Justice!"

"Lied about what?"

"Guns. He was going to allow Columbia, Missouri, he said, to ban assault weapons. He understood, he also said, the true meaning of the first clause of the Second Amendment. You must have heard about the case, how Cavendish and the Court ruled."

"Yes, more or less. But, of course, I didn't know what he had told you privately."

"I tried talking sense to him, as did the Chief Justice. He won't retire! ... Here's the part I haven't mentioned. We have disqualifying evidence against him, but he refutes it, laughs in our faces, the SOB!"

"How disqualifying?"

"Rape, after which his rich Daddy paid for an abortion."

"Were charges brought? I'm thinking about the existence of any court proceedings."

"Apparently, they handled it quietly, but there's no mistaking his guilt. We have a copy of the affidavit filed by the young woman, an affidavit from the doctor who performed the abortion, and a statement from a lawyer friend of Cavendish in Houston who knows the whole sordid story. Claims he was at the frat party—orgy—where it went down."

"If I'm going to help you, I must have a guarantee of anonymity. How would you handle that ... if, of course, I should agree to help you?"

"I have no way to do that, Dave, no guarantee to offer of any kind. But I will tell you that I wouldn't know who had knowledge of any plan, were there one. Maybe it's best we forget the whole thing, forget I called. Oh, and get rid of that phone!"

"Just so you know, Madam President, the 'special' agent would simply get an untraceable, coded text message with a photo on his phone. He would not know who hired him or the reason. These guys are robot-like, not thinkers, not philosophers. I might even venture they don't have the same human feelings as you and me."

"Is that what we're doing right now, Dave, having human feelings?"

"I suppose not. But should you change your mind, I don't want to know, so, don't call me again. I am going to send you an encrypted phone number, again, just in case. You've got plenty of codebreakers at your disposal, but if I were you, I'd have anyone who breaks this encrypted number disappeared. You've got plenty of those types as well. Nice talking to you, Gloria … Oops, I forgot. 'Madam President.'"

THIRTY

"I want to go to Camp David this weekend, Sean. I've got some thinking to do, and I don't need distractions … distractions beyond the ordinary."

"Yes, Ma'am. Will you be needing a chief of staff?" he asked, knowing full well the answer. "You'll need the 'football.'"

"Yes, both, of course. Perhaps when I'm tired of thinking we could play some gin rummy or poker. Just make sure we've got enough matches!"

Sean had been looking forward to Gloria's next weekend at Camp David. He had something on his mind, something he'd harbored quietly for years but could not speak or act on out of respect for their years of friendship and her title. Now, however, he believed if he didn't speak or act soon, the flame he had felt would burn out.

Could 'gin rummy,' 'poker,' 'matches' have been metaphors for other activities? Were the words a simple code between the two of them, perhaps? Was Gloria hinting at something? He wanted it to be so. Desperately.

♠

Camp David was a rustic, presidential getaway in Maryland's Catoctin Mountain Park, a thirty-minute helicopter ride from the White House. Constructed by the CCC in the 1930s, every president since Franklin Roosevelt had used it. FDR dubbed it 'Shangri-La.' Perhaps that was the 'Shangri-La' the president meant when the press asked him the origin of the Doolittle Raid on Japan in 1942. Dwight Eisenhower changed the name in honor of his grandson.

Whatever the name and whichever the president, the retreat offered the chief executive and his guests a soothing atmosphere for contemplation or, depending on the ages and enthusiasm of the president and his or her guests, a plethora of indoor and outdoor activities.

When the president goes to Camp David or anywhere outside the White House, a military aide carrying a heavy black briefcase follows. The briefcase is commonly known as the 'nuclear football' or simply the 'football.' Hence Sean McKinnon's reference to it when President Addison announced her intention. The 'football' contained the codes the president needed to launch a U.S. response to an enemy attack.

♠

After an unusually jarring helicopter ride with Sean and her aide with the 'football,' President Addison settled into Aspen Lodge, the building set aside for the president. She changed into her bathing suit, noticing that it had become a little tight, nodded her acceptance—she wasn't going to change her lifestyle now—and walked the few yards down to the outdoor pool. She asked the staff not to disturb her with requests for food or drink, especially phone calls; she wanted absolute privacy. Sean McKinnon understood his presence wouldn't be necessary until his boss was ready. He had already been looking forward to a horseback ride.

Gloria adjusted her snorkel and mask—coating the inside of the glass with spit to prevent fogging—and began slowly to work into her normal stroke and breathing rhythm. It wasn't a lap pool, but with the vision her mask provided she managed to remain above an imaginary centerline of the figure-eight shaped facility.

She didn't need the exercise, but she knew this was the only way to blot out everything but her own thoughts. It was the greatest way to unclutter her mind she'd ever found! Better than walking, jogging, or cycling. Fewer physical obstacles.

She had one thing on her mind: Justice Randolph Cavendish. Truth be known, she didn't believe it hadn't been worth the effort to get him on the bench, to say nothing of his betrayal on the Second. But it was necessary. As she stroked along, she couldn't get Dave Charles out of her mind. She thought of it as the 'Charles solution.' She was no dummy; she knew what an encrypted message meant.

'Am I a moral person?' she asked herself.

She was sure the answer was 'yes,' with qualification.

'Was one qualification murder?'

'No!' Murder was not.'

'Is having someone killed worth the price? Could I get away with it, and if I did, live with myself? I'm not sure.'

'When I'm caught, for there was a better than even chance that I would, what would it do to the party? Forget that! To the country? Was Randolph Cavendish worth any of that? No, he was just another little man with an oversized sense of self-importance. I'm the President of the United States! I may be small, but I know who I am, and that's not pretense! …

'S**t! What the hell am I doing? This swim was supposed to free my mind of crap like that!'

♠

The swimmer reached the shallow end of the pool, waded out, and toweled off.

Back in Aspen, she started to wiggle out of her one-piece bathing suit in front of the bathroom mirror. She noticed how certain body parts jiggled and stopped for a moment to examine herself. She lifted her breasts to see what effect age had on them.

'Hmmm … Forty-one and no kids. So, not bad.'

There was something about the head-clearing swim—and touching her breasts— that suddenly infused her with longing. She donned one of the monogrammed, white terry-cloth robes. She told the secret service detail she would be playing poker with Mr. McKinnon and they needn't worry about her the rest of the night.

"Do not disturb me for any reason. *Any reason! Capiche?*"

She would have good reason to wonder later why what happened next happened.

♠

"Did she have anything on under that robe, Tom?"

The speaker was Special Agent Robert Skinner, junior to Tom Lester. Skinner told him not to worry about it. He wasn't smiling when he spoke.

Minutes later, as if drawn by some irresistible force, Gloria found herself at Sean's cabin door wondering what the hell she was doing. But there she was, so, she knocked gently.

"Madam President! Come in, please."

As he closed the door, she put her hand on his forearm. When he'd closed the door, he placed his hand on hers.

She reached up with her free hand to the side of his neck, pulled him gently down, and kissed him sweetly on the lips. Neither said anything.

One need not have a powerful imagination to guess what went through Sean McKinnon's mind at that moment.

But what she did next was definitely not 'gin rummy' or 'poker,' or any other coded activity. Nope, it was seduction, plain and simple.

The President of the United States stepped back a pace and loosed her robe, bending her left knee to her right, rotating her hips in the same direction and turning her upper torso to give her erstwhile lover a profile of breasts unadulterated by a child. She took his right hand and placed it on her left breast. The nipple hardened against his palm and tingled her moistening vagina, as though a child was feeding, she imagined. Then, she reached down ...

♠

When they had satisfied themselves, both fell fast asleep until around12:30 A.M. What had happened earlier now seemed a blur.

She sat up and started straightening her hair. He watched, still astonished.

"I can't wait until you ruminate about your next victim," he teased.

"Screw you!" she laughed. "Don't get your hopes up for a repeat performance, Sean McKinnon! Now, get out your cards and matches. I'm in that certain mood, well known to all us tough and horny broads, and I know when I've got a winning hand!"

"The smile on your face and your earlier … 'confidence'? Would that be the right word for it? Tells me you've solved your problem."

"Shut up and deal! I can always change my mood, if you get my drift."

"Where's your ante, Madam President?"

"What's the ante?"

"Ten … But what you decided out there in the pool, and why, I might consider an acceptable substitute."

The President of the United States, who felt that her opportunity to relax and Camp David had allowed her to grow a couple of inches. Still wearing an open robe, counted out ten matches and pushed them to the middle of the table.

Then, she spread open the five cards in her hand. Never the one to wear a 'poker face,' known to all who played poker in Columbus or worked at Cummins, she smiled reflexively at her cards.

"You know, 'Madam President,'" Sean smiled wickedly as he mocked her title, "if Clinton Downey had seen your face just now, you would never have become president."

THIRTY-ONE

"What the f**k?"

McKinnon's vocal reaction to loud knocking at the cabin door was classic.

The President of the United States pushed back her chair, closed her robe and fled toward the master bathroom. Her losing hand fell ignominiously to the floor.

McKinnon found Tom Lester and Robert Skinner at the door. Both showed an unusual state of agitation.

"Is the president here?" Lester demanded. His tone suggested that McKinnon had better not lie.

"What's happening?" Gloria said as she walked from the bathroom toward the door. She was wearing ill-fitting clothes pulled hastily from Sean's closet. Lester and Skinner looked at each other and smiled.

"Well," she demanded. "And you don't need to be smirking and giggling around me. What you should be doing is thanking Mr. McKinnon for saving my life."

"What?" Tom Lester blurted out. "Saved your life? Just how did he do that?"

"I wanted to relax after my swim, so, I took an Ambien, for getting that I was also having a martini. I got lightheaded, stood, and promptly fell into the pool. Fortunately, Mr. McKinnon wandered by just then and saw me floating face down. He pulled me out and resuscitated me, remembering what he'd learned as a Scout back in Columbus."

"And you're sticking with that story, Ma'am?"

"Yes, I am, Tom, as are you and Robert. Is that clear?

The two agents shared another smirk.

"I said, is that clear?"

"Crystal," Lester replied.

"Robert?"

"Crystal clear, Madam President," Skinner repeated, "but shouldn't you be seen by your doctor?"

The president let that pass with a withering stare at the junior agent.

"Now, gentlemen, what the hell are you doing here? I specifically asked for complete privacy."

"We have some bad news, Madam President," Lester answered. Phil Thompson died this evening in a Beltway car crash."

Thompson was Addison's transportation secretary, and the Beltway a freeway that encircled the capitol.

"Oh, s**t! Okay, fellas. I appreciate your bringing me the news. Now, if you'll excuse me, I need to talk to Maxine Thompson. Robert, please get me Mrs. Thompson on the phone in my cabin."

"Do you think they bought it, Sean?" Addison asked her lover as her detail set off briskly for Aspen Lodge.

"Would you?" he replied.

♠

President Addison spent most of an hour on the telephone with Maxine Thompson. Gloria was genuinely sad for the Thompson family who she had known since Phil Thompson's becoming mayor of Buffalo, New York, two terms ago. She wanted him for transportation because she knew from experience that mayors were hands-on people; they must be; the complaints stopped with them. Midwestern mayors were familiar with moving people and goods around their cities during periods of the worst weather imaginable. Buffalo and Phil Thompson were no strangers to that!

How ironic, she mused later, that Thompson, the transportation secretary, died on one of his highways.

♠

THIRTY-TWO

August 14. Two days before the anniversary of *Hendricks*.

Paul Vanni rubbed his eyes in disbelief.

He wasn't sure, but he recognized a photo on his phone of someone vaguely familiar.

In the years since his first 'hit,' the accidental one for his landlady that hadn't started with murderous intent, his career had grown, not blossomed but had also not been static.

When he sat up in bed and turned on the nightstand light next to him, he awakened the figure in the other half of their queen-sized bed who wasn't thrilled to see that it was 3:34 A.M.

"What's going on, Paul. Don't you see what time it is?" she grumbled.

"Sorry, Eunice, I just received an important text, and I'm trying with the light on to make sure I understand it. I'll turn it off in a second."

True to his word, Vanni turned off the light, but sleep escaped him. The photo on his phone haunted him. It appeared to be the first such assignment. He hadn't many assignments, but he retrieved all of them from one of the encryption methods used by various underworld figures.

Each sponsor provided a unique symbol that identified him or her to the recipient (asset); an inverted 'A,' for example, or in another example a reversed 'C' with a bar above, below, or above and below. This assignment told him the sponsor was someone in a position that required the highest level of security—anonymity. On top of that, the photo had come across encrypted. He'd had only two prior encrypted assignments.

Previously, from advice he read in a bookstore copy of *Wired*, he found a computer whiz who recommended a half-dozen decoding programs. The young man was positive, he told Paul, that one of them would work on any known encryption. Two plus two did not equal four, Paul decided, it equaled the government.

He tried to confirm his suspicion after breakfast with Eunice. She left around 8:30 A.M. for work at Costco where she was a checker, and Paul began rummaging through their apartment for something that would jog his memory or better yet directly reveal the subject's identity.

Certainty of a target's identity was central to his 'jobs.' No one was going to reward him for murdering the wrong person. The information left for him at a drop left no doubt about identity. The one on his phone, which he'd unscrambled when it came in, required guesswork and research.

He began to ransack the apartment. Closets, cabinets, drawers, under the couch cushions—he even looked in the dishwasher. He knew he'd seen that face! He didn't really know what he was looking for, a face, somewhere, but he continued, nonetheless. While he searched, the TV on the kitchen counter blared the news, over and over, same news, all day, non-stop.

Exhausted after nearly an hour of sleuthing, he plopped down in the chair Eunice normally occupied next to the couch. He lit a cigarette to relax, which was the only time he smoked, and looked for the ashtray that normally sat on the arm of the couch. When it wasn't there, he looked down between the couch and Eunice's chair. Staring back at him was a messy stack of old newspapers and magazines.

He stood and picked up the pile, tossing one after the another onto the couch. Near the bottom of the stack a two-week-old copy of *Time.* The person in his phone now smiled up at him.

'That's who they want killed! What the f**k!

The revelation shook Paul Vanni's confidence as no other assignment had. Unable to control his legs and feeling faint, he grabbed the armrest and guided himself back into Eunice's chair. Two minutes later Paul Vanni was fast asleep.

Eunice Walker returned from her shift at Costco about 4:30 P.M. Almost immediately she saw that someone had cleaned the apartment, top to bottom. Bed made;

dishes washed and put away; floors mopped or vacuumed; toilet cleaned! Whenever he'd done that last one it nearly took her breath away.

"Paul?" she called, "are you here?"

Just then he followed her through the door.

"Hi, honey. Saw you drive up. I just walked over to the 7-Eleven for more cigarettes. How was work?"

"Tiring. You know, it always amazes me how much stuff people take out of there. I'll swear there's a lot of hoarding going on in this town ...

"So, I see you did some cleaning, for which I am grateful, but does it mean you're off on one of those 'assignments' of yours? It would be a good sign for the future of our relationship if someday you told me about them."

"You know I can't do that, Baby."

"You say it's secret government work, but you don't seem to know that much about the government."

"Let's forget it. I'll call you when I've settled in. I can tell you this much, I'm going all the way to the West Coast. I'll need you to drive me to JFK in the morning."

"What time's your flight?"

"We need to be there at 5:00. Flight is at 6:10."

"Show me your ticket."

"Not ticketed yet. I'll do that at the check-in counter in the morning."

She knew he was lying. Not the first time, but she held her tongue. She was clever enough to know eventually the truth will out.

'What was the job this time?' She hoped it would pay better than the last.

♠

Paul hauled himself out of the car at 4:55 the next morning. He picked up his small duffel bag, waved, and turned toward the departure terminal and the ticketing lines inside.

Through the large windows of the terminal, he watched Eunice drive off. When she made the turn toward the freeway, Paul exited the terminal and hailed a taxi.

"Where to, pal?"

"Penn Station."

The cabby, a Pakistani, he figured, tried to make small talk along the way, but Paul did his best to ignore him. He figured the least he had to say about anything the better. One slip might give someone the ability to find him afterwards.

The cabby had grown silent before they reached the terminal. Paul gave him a small tip and went inside to find the Flixbus ticket window.

The bus fare to Washington, about fifty bucks, turned out to be less than the cab fare from JFK to Penn Station, which disgusted Paul. He was certain the cabby had cheated him when he refused to respond to the man's incessant chatter, most of which he found to be unintelligible rants about his family, city politics, and the regulations imposed on cabbies. So, he reduced the usual tip by half out of spite.

♠

THIRTY-THREE

Senator Hiram Westfield checked his calendar for a conflict and saw none. He picked up his phone—by now the kind of phone and its purpose was obvious—and punched in a number. When he heard the familiar voice on the other end, he had only one thing in mind.

"Did you send it?" he asked in a demanding manner.

The junior senator from South Dakota answered in the affirmative.

"Take it easy, Senator, it's done."

Senator Stephen Brook collapsed onto his office couch, still clutching the phone, although the call had ended. He had mixed feelings about what he had just set in motion at the bidding of another. He earnestly believed what they had done together was for the good of the country—a much-overused cliché—but he also knew it would mean someone's life, perhaps many lives. Even a civil war. Why Stephen Brook should care about lives lost, even in a small way, or why he so willingly took orders from someone else, testified to ... It testified to nothing. It was simply inexplicable.

After a few minutes of contemplation, which settled zilch in Brook's mind about the propriety of his action, he rose from the couch and returned the phone to its place behind a stack of newspapers in his office bookcase. Anyone watching him would see that he moved without enthusiasm.

♠

Early in life, Stephen Brook, of Custer, South Dakota, wanted to be, as badly as anyone could want to be, a professional rodeo cowboy. He wanted it so bad it hurt, hurt in a very different way than finding himself thrown unceremoniously from a bucking bronc or a brahma bull. Nonetheless, the point when he had to be realistic about his future—he also wanted a family—occurred when the wannabe rodeo-star-turned-politician was much, much younger.

He had managed to pay his way through the University of Wyoming on those youthful rodeo earnings before his bones became brittle. His education, however, for better or worse elevated his sights in a different direction, helped along by his broken bones and the prospect of even more. What he learned—not from his professors, one must say in their defense—what he came to believe in Laramie was an extraordinarily perverse sense, an inverse sense most people would believe, that the opportunity of a fine education had deprived him of what he really wanted out of life—rodeo stardom. (Later, as a senator, he strutted around the Capitol in his signature Stetson). Education had made of Stephen Brook a victim. It had taken from him his identity. At Laramie, he met another future senator with his own sense of victimhood, the Svengali-like, Hiram Westfield.

In the Senate, the man from Lusk, Wyoming, would make of Stephen Brook a susceptible protégé in whom he could locate a political ideology, which, at its core was an instinctive hatred of the opposite party, its programs, and a demonization of its practitioners.

♠

How Westfield himself arrived at the same view wasn't entirely clear. He'd had every advantage growing up, but something happened along the way that filled him with seething anger at nearly everything and everybody. One could speculate that he'd experienced some life-changing event, the kind that leaves a person enfolded within an impenetrable mold. Perhaps an angry and violent father? A betrayal of some kind? Perhaps it was as simple as the fact he just didn't like folks from the opposite party. But precisely who, when, or what no one could say, not even Westfield most probably.

Normally, an angry man couldn't get elected dog catcher. But Wyoming was a large state of small towns spread far apart in which reputations went unnoticed by just enough people unaware of a Svengali in their midst—even the meaning of Svengali. Hiram Westfield's politics came down to this: in all things political, the end justified the means. That simple equation had always proved attractive to those who didn't know what questions to ask or didn't want to bother to ask.

♠

Men like Westfield and Brook believed they had an obligation to defend the Second Amendment *beyond* a defense of the Constitution itself. The Second *was* the Constitution. 'Domestic enemies,' against whom senators and others swore to fight, included those who did not believe the amendment provided for unrestricted gun ownership and the right to carry weapons ('bear') anywhere. The senators, obsessed with their own point of view called opponents of the amendment traitors, and in so doing stretched the definition of treason beyond its legal boundaries: they were 'domestic enemies,' a category that included the President of the United States.

What solution (end) did Westfield and Brook propose? Quite simple, really, quite logical if one accepts the paramountcy of the Second. Opponents of the amendment as interpreted in *Hendricks* had committed treason against the United States:

> Whoever, owing allegiance to the United States, levies war against them or adheres to their enemies, giving them aid and comfort within the United States or elsewhere, is guilty of treason and shall suffer death, or shall be imprisoned not less than five years and fined under this title but not less than $10,000; and shall be

incapable of holding any office under the United States, 18 U.S. Code § 2381.

The means to the senators' end? The men of standing need not dirty their hands, they believed. They, the men of standing, would leave the method of execution to vigilantes, society's marginalized and disillusioned. Men who had no real stake in outcomes, who took orders rather than giving them. Men with a profound sense of societal inversion and personal victimhood who were determined to find a way to strike back. Men for whom the carrying out of revenge was far more satisfying than the restoration itself. Men who had nothing to lose. Men very much in the mold of a Paul Vanni or a Clinton Downey.

♠

THIRTY-FOUR

At the president's insistence, her Secret Service detail nearly always included the two special agents who headed the assignment at Camp David, Tom Lester and Bob Skinner. Of the two, Lester, the service's senior special agent for protection, led Addison's detail everywhere she went outside the White House, his time off the only exception.

♠

Tom Lester and Bob Skinner's ascendance to special agent status was probably more difficult than Gloria

Addison's to the presidency: the Secret Service accepted fewer than 1 percent of special agent applicants.

Both special agents had bachelor's degrees in criminal justice, Lester from the University of Oregon and Skinner from Ohio State University. Prior to their applications to the Service, both men had spent time on the police forces of their respective communities, Portland and Cincinnati.

Both men were married with young children. The camaraderie of Service families was like that of families on military bases around the country, although Service families, insulated to be sure, lived within civilian communities. The Lester's and Skinner's were part of a large, tight-knit organization, supportive of each other in all respects.

Tom and Bob would begin their potential Service careers as prospective field agents. The first set of criteria was easy: American citizens, a valid driver's license, excellent health and physical condition, visual acuity no worse than 20/100 uncorrected or correctable to 20/20 in each eye', and age twenty-one to thirty. Eligible military veterans could apply past age thirty-seven. Those for starters!

Having met those criteria, the Service required them to complete a ten-step program in two phases.

Phase one began with a résumé review, in-depth interviews, drug screening, medical diagnoses, a full-scope polygraph examination, written exam, a test of their physical abilities, an interview, and a *conditional* job offer.

Phase two included a security and credit check, another polygraph test, medical and psychological exams, and a background check that took up to nine months. Applicants also needed to be well-rounded, which meant they must demonstrate extensive weapons and water survival skills.

Both men qualified in all Phase One and Phase Two criteria. Then came one more hurdle: their pasts. The use of any illegal drugs after age twenty-three meant automatic disqualification. They wondered, of course, how the Service could determine that. The same result applied if either had bought or sold drugs at any time in their lives. Again, Tom and Bob had no idea how the Service would know this.

Finally, they faced a hiring panel for a decision on hiring. Obviously, the Service hired both men.

♠

If Tom and Bob were ambitious enough to reach the upper echelon of the Service, they would discover that their employer selected only the best from the crop of field agents to be special agents. For Tom Lester and Bob Skinner, as it was for any member of the president's protective detail, the progression toward that end had begun with six to eight years at an assigned field office. It was a frustrating and agonizing apprenticeship.

Before that night at Camp David, both special agents expected to spend three to five years in their current protective assignment, then round out their careers at a field office or at service headquarters in Washington.

That was *before*. Now, they supposed the president might have something to say about their tenure and retirement.

♠

THIRTY-FIVE

August 15. One day before the anniversary of *Hendricks*: Clinton Downey rolled out of bed just before daylight. He'd had a rough night. Fitful sleep. Dreams he couldn't reconstruct altogether. Just that he was falling. Bad dreams.

Before he put on the coffee, he opened the closet door and pulled the light cord.

'Yes!' he exclaimed silently. Still there.

Not entirely satisfied, however, he bent down and slid a camouflaged duffel bag into to the bedroom. Down on his haunches, he didn't open the bag but patted and stroked its contents along its length, apparently making sure that what he expected to be there was there. The movement of his hands, however, resulted in metallic clunking sounds from inside, louder than he expected. Whatever the bag held had shifted. Alarmed, he stopped and looked up, as though he were listening for something. When, apparently, he heard nothing more than the light rain that had been falling most of the night, he exhaled and quietly closed the door, or as quietly as he could, forgetting to turn out the light.

Clinton Downey's mind was a swirling mix of conspiracies, all of them centered on the idea that the 'world' was out to squash the ambition of Clinton Downey. That world had narrowed to *his* world, a world within reach, a world that found him 'enslaved' by those privileged enough to work for the U.S. government.

Was it rational to believe that those who attacked the Second Amendment were responsible for all that had happened to Downey over the years? Of course, not. But rationality was never the point in a mind warped by years of frustration, futility and failure.

Now, Clinton Downey believed he alone understood the elitist manipulation of the system, an atmosphere that reeked of how to put down those like himself. Tucked away in that duffel bag Downey possessed the power to make himself whole. Someone in his head told him so, told him what he could do, told him the end of abuse had to begin somewhere.

♠

By the time Downey had gone over his grievances for the umpteenth time, stoking his anger and grinding his teeth, the weather over Washington had cleared. The early morning overcast and light drizzle had turned to partly cloudy, the blue sky broken occasionally by small cumulus clouds, the kind that children and imaginative adults would exclaim they resembled popcorn or cotton candy or something else of their fancy.

He smiled. Tomorrow the air would be clear of everything.

♠

THIRTY-SIX

The weather on the morning of the 15th mattered less to the president and congressional leaders. Theirs was a protest that must take place regardless of the weather. The president felt buoyant. Perhaps it was the change in the forecast.

The rally in opposition to *Hendricks* the next day would be a feel-good event but a dangerous one. Although she was not sure she would attend, Addison nonetheless looked forward to it in spirit. She met with the majority leader and the speaker of the house, as well as the chiefs of the Metropolitan and Capitol police.

Everyone in the Oval Office anticipated a counter or counter demonstration, quite possibly a violent one.

The NRA leadership would be there, she was sure, stirring up the assemblage with its shop-worn, provocative rhetoric—'the only way to stop a bad guy with a gun is a good guy with a gun.' Militias would temporarily abandon their secretive, wooded compounds for the city. To the police officers present, she emphasized the necessity to anticipate where violence could erupt and be prepared to close any corresponding gaps in their defenses.

"Stan," the president addressed the Metropolitan police chief, Stanley Shaw, informally. "I'd like you to brief our congressional leadership about guns in the District. Something tells me there will be plenty around. Members are attending the protest at the Court."

"Yes, of course, Madam President. To begin, the District requires a license to carry a concealed handgun or to have a loaded handgun in a vehicle. My department has issued licenses to qualified applicants, residents and non-residents, on a 'shall issue' basis. Concealed carry licenses issued by other jurisdictions are not valid here. That would most certainly be the case for the militias."

"What the hell does 'shall issue' mean?" Senator Clark wondered impatiently. The speaker looked at Chief Shaw in a manner suggesting he was curious as well.

"It means that so long as you pass the basic state requirements, the issuing authority—that's my department—*shall issue* you a permit. The alternative is a 'may issue' permit, which means that when you pass the basic requirements the issuing authority *may issue* you a permit—not *shall* ...

"What are the *shall issue* parameters?" Speaker Jackson Burrows asked.

"Generally, they include an age restriction, firearms safety training, fingerprinting, a passport-style photograph, the possibility of a background check, and any past criminal record … I can be more specific, if you wish, gentlemen."

"Yes, Chief, if you please," the president intervened.

"In addition to the requirements I already mentioned, applicants must declare the address for each firearm. Non-residents, with a place of business or employment in the District may register a firearm maintained at that place of business or employment ...

"Handgun registrants must be at least twenty-one; long guns 18–21 with a qualified adult co-registering. We limit handgun models to any of those appearing on one of the California, Massachusetts, Maryland or D.C. Police 'approved rosters' by make/model. We control long guns by an allowed/not-allowed attributes list ...

"We confirm your information. If it checks out, you get a permit. Now, you can be sure there will be hundreds of people at the protest who have neither kind of permit, *shall issue* or *may issue*."

Senator Clark inquired about concealed weapons.

"*May issue* states, which we are not by law, usually require you to provide a reason to carry concealed: fear for your life or safety, or that of your family. *May issue* states, therefore, are more restrictive than *shall issue* states, because the issuing authority has a say as to whether you get a permit or not."

"And open carry, Stan?" the president asked.

"The District does not allow 'open carry,' except by law enforcement, military servicemembers, and security professionals engaged in their official duties ...

"Under an 'Enhanced Penalty Provision,' District law declared areas 1,000 feet from a school, college, day care center, playground, library, public housing complex and other public gathering spots as enhanced penalty zones. The Metropolitan Police Department has clarified that this restriction acts only as a penalty enhancement for gun *crimes* within 1,000 feet of those locations ...

"The District cannot ban handguns; that was one point of *Hendricks,* and it's one reason for the protest. Beyond that, as you know, the Court ruled that the Second Amendment acknowledges and guarantees the right of the individual to possess and carry firearms in the United States. *Period.*"

♠

Clinton Downey had arrived in Washington the day before behind the wheel of a Ford F150 pickup. He checked into a one-star hotel, the D.C. International Hostel, on 7th Street Northwest in Mount Vernon Square, which was no more than a 30-minute walk from the Supreme Court.

♠

That same day Paul Vanni checked into another cheap hotel, the Duo Nomad, a few blocks behind (east) the Capitol and Supreme Court.

♠

THIRTY-SEVEN

"Stephen, meet me tomorrow at 'Medium Rare.' It's more out of the way than most places for lunch, and we can talk candidly with some confidence of privacy."

"What time, Hy?"

"12:30."

♠

'Medium Rare' was a popular Congressional lunch and dinner spot located at a place Washingtonians called 'Barracks Row.' The latter was the oldest commercial area in the D.C. near the Navy Yard. Since the turn of the century, the northern end of the strip had seen a rejuvenation after decades of decline, but a freeway presented a barrier to further development.

Both senators arrived at 'Medium Rare' simultaneously and settled into the most isolated booth. Brook uncharacteristically doffed his signature Stetson and set in on the seat next to him. One might guess he did so to protect their secrecy. Both were nervous … more interested in talking than eating. They had plenty to discuss.

"When do you expect the demonstrations at the Court to begin?" Westfield asked.

"I believe the peak will occur about 3:00 P.M. when our guys explain the virtues of *Hendricks*. That result will bring out all the craziness from the crazies on the other side. But as far as people demonstrating, they'll be there from early morning."

♠

Stephen Brook hadn't known what to expect when he sat down. Thus far the burden for 'where things stood' had been on him. He knew the man across the table could be impatient and volatile. He put his lips around the straw and drew a mouthful of his iced tea as he considered how to answer.

He was confident in the plan, and he wanted to convey that to Westfield. But common sense and history told him no plan was foolproof. There were always one or two things, if you're lucky, that will go wrong no matter how hard you've worked to achieve a flawless result.

"Are we ready? Is our guy ready?"

"Honestly, Hiram, who knows? Everything is in place, but we picked a marginal character to execute it. This I do know: our guy is in place."

Brook did not want to sound overly optimistic. He didn't think it would work with the older man.

"What about the bus station?"

"That, too."

"Is there anything, anything at all, to connect either of us to your guy?"

"No! I'm just a voice on a phone."

"Why did he agree to do it … to a 'voice on a phone'? Not because you're a senator. Obviously."

"Money. Loves the Second. Hates … fears what the president will do to it …

"Look, if things go south, and they catch and squeeze him, no one would believe a senator had hired him. He has no way of knowing that. So, to involve me he'd have to concoct a story so farfetched nobody could possibly believe him about anything. There's no physical evidence that ties him to me. And as for you? You can't possibly exist in his world."

"You're absolutely sure there's no physical tie to either of us?"

"A sure as one can be, Senator."

They finished their lunch and took a cab together back to their offices in the Hart building. They continued to discuss their plans along the way.

"Will you be going back to Lusk?"

"Hell, no! That'd be something the overly curious would find suspicious. I'm going to quietly dismiss my staff and go over to Georgetown to see 'my girl.'"

Brook was no stranger, of course, to politicians' references to their 'girls.' No one imagined they meant their children or their wives.

"And you, Stephen? How you gonna spend the rest of that momentous day?"

Despite the confident bonhomie at lunch and in the taxi, was Hiram Westfield really convinced his colleague had sufficiently covered their tracks if the authorities caught their man? Sufficiently enough so if the cops did break their man, he could only give them 'number one and number two.' But what could he do about the level of sufficiency now, at the last moment?

Westfield's executive assistant momentarily interrupted his growing worry.

"I assume you won't be attending the protest tomorrow, Senator?"

♠

As soon as Stewart Denny mentioned tomorrow's protest, he knew it was a mistake. A BIG mistake.

His innocent reminder of the event nearly caused Westfield to explode. He remained silent a few moments before answering, fearful that he might say something or reveal something by his mood that later someone might construe as suspicious. He finally answered, trying not to sound as angry on the outside as Denny had made him feel on the inside.

"No, Stewart, I won't be attending" he said simply and calmly.

Stewart tried to make amends.

"Did you have a pleasant lunch, Senator?"

"Yes, yes, a fine lunch, thank you."

Stewart could see that his boss's mind was elsewhere. He wondered what had happened during that lunch to alter Westfield's morning affability. He decided not to press the senator further.

Westfield reached the same conclusion. He intended to do as he'd told Brook. Georgetown. History would take care of the rest while he enjoyed himself.

"What's next, Stewart? I need to get busy with policies that matter instead of thinking about what the other side is doing every minute."

Stewart thought a little levity, standard office sarcasm, might relax his boss.

"Well, Senator, there is always the fun stuff: federal versus public lands. And when we get tired and frustrated with those, we can take another look at water rights."

Westfield smiled and patted Stewart's shoulder.

"I'll say this for you, Stewart. You sure know how to cheer a fellow up. Public lands and water rights. Wow! Better than another dessert! Now, get out of here. I've got some thinking to do."

♠

Senator Brook's afternoon differed slightly but significantly still from that of his co-conspirator. Doubtless, his more direct involvement in their joint project would have left him even more unsettled than Westfield. There it was. 'Unsettled.'

'That meant guilt, didn't it?'

He decided to leave early for a good, stiff drink with his wife at their home in Chevy Chase, Maryland. Perhaps that form of relaxation out on their screened porch would clear his mind of the anxiety—yet another word for guilt—eating at him. Just the thought of his wife and that drink began the soothing process he craved.

As soon as he nestled into their rocking divan across from Cheryl Brook, however, his thoughts turned dark again as he realized he was betraying the woman he loved, the woman whose goodness, decency and support whenever he stumbled had kept him afloat during 23 years of marriage and two Senate campaigns.

For a second or two he wanted to grab that phone secreted away in his office bookcase and call off the whole thing. But no, some things were just too important. So, he sat there with his gin and tonic, and smiled at Cheryl, knowing that his great purpose in life might blow up her world along with his.

'They won't catch me, and I will have served my country.'

He smiled again at his wife and finished his first gin and tonic. He intended to get drunk. *That* would stop the voices.

THIRTY-EIGHT

Paul Vanni had experienced another difficult night. Following the recent rain, it was unseasonably humid, even for Washington ... muggy. He hadn't dared turn on the air conditioner in his room. He tried it once and found it so loud he knew he'd never be able to sleep.

Because of Duo Nomad's location in an undesirable (crime-infested) section of Washington, management had barred the windows of every room on the outside and locked them with a special key on the inside. He might not be able to breathe, but the thought that no one could possibly find him accorded Vanni a small measure of compensation.

So, Vanni suffered through hours of nightmares (falling or jumping from a high place), watching television, sweating, or lying awake. He finally fell asleep, free of all nightmares, around 5:00 A.M.

Three hours later an outside noise jolted him awake. The sound was two people arguing in the parking lot. He was too sleepy to catch their words, but from all appearances he expected it to become violent at any moment. He considered alerting the desk clerk but decided it was none of his business and the clerk likely knew of it already. Besides, the last thing he needed today was a distraction, particularly one that would throw of his timing.

He took a quick shower and shaved. The day he arrived he'd noticed a Denny's restaurant about three blocks from his hotel/motel. He liked Denny's. Their menu rarely changed. Reliable in every sense. You could always count on having exactly what you wanted no matter where you found one of their franchises. That variation of the classic obsessive/compulsive disorder was very reassuring to Paul Vanni who saw a world mostly in disarray.

He sat for breakfast and ordered his favorite, the 'Grand Slam Slugger': two buttermilk pancakes, two eggs, two bacon strips, two sausage links served with hash browns or choice of bread, plus coffee and juice. He told the waitress that he'd like both the potatoes and the bread, but could she make it an English muffin?

The middle-aged woman finished writing, stuck her pencil behind her ear, smacked her chewing gum and took his menu.

"You got it, honey," she said casually as she walked to the orders counter and slipped his behind a clip above.

He didn't think much of her attempt at familiarity but figured she was the sort that called every customer 'honey.'

When he'd finished, he felt stuffed, but it was a satisfying feeling.

Back at Duo Nomad he turned on the television. The news carried a story, probably made up, he believed, that the president might attend tomorrow's Court protest.

He let out a loud 'Humph! There they go, again, how typical, reporting something they had no clue about. He, Paul Vanni, knew better. His client had assured him the president *would* appear, perhaps make a few remarks.

Of this he was certain. The client had secreted the payoff at an agreed drop, a locker in the downtown Greyhound station. Once the client was satisfied with the result, Downey would find the key to that locker in a FedEx envelope waiting for him at one of their outlets.

He hadn't done business with this client before, so it all boiled down to a matter of trust. He had no reason to doubt the client; it was reassuring that he could associate the caller's number in Washington with someone in the government. When he considered just who in the nation's capital might wish to harm the president, he half exhaled, half whistled —whew! That number had to be astronomical.

♠

Not far from the Duo Nomad, Clinton Downey stared at the TV in his room. His mind, however, unlike his eyes, was not watching the programming that normally interested him—'The Price is Right' and the like.

One could cut him some slack for that bit of absentmindedness given the weight of his circumstance.

Because of his interest in game show programing, if not its actual presentation, Downey missed the announcement of the president's change of mind that had briefly entertained Paul Vanni. And that was a bit odd, considering their past political history, his and the president's—testimony, perhaps, to the power of television to dumb down viewers?

Clinton Downey did, however, vaguely sense as he sat there that his obsession to defend the Second Amendment had prevented him from constructing a thorough plan to carry out his reason for being in Washington and managing its aftermath—avoiding discovery.

Thoughts of escape included a consideration of Mexico, but he didn't have a passport, which also eliminated any flight out of the country. Then, oddly, but doubtless triggered by considerations of safe passage out of Washington, he recalled the film with Humphrey Bogart in which, after a botched robbery, Bogie flees into the mountains. He knew from all the crime films he'd seen that when a man climbed up, he was doomed. Even Bogie.

'What was the title?' he wracked his brain without result. 'Oh well, damn good movie. Bogie showed himself to the lawmen's guns to save a dog, and they plugged him. Damn! Typical.'

He mused for a few moments on the tragedy of Bogie's plight, a weak man in the crunch, then returned to the job ahead. He'd be sure not to climb up anything.

♠

Following breakfast on the 15th, Paul Vanni checked out of the Duo Nomad, rented a car and made his way to Capitol Hill to put the final touches on his plan. He spent most of the day searching for a rooming house. The few available candidates required a minimum of two weeks or a month, which he was happy to settle for because he believed it would be safter that his landlord, facing possible questioning, would have the impression he planned to rent longer than one night. Nonetheless, the most important aspect to his success at finding a room was having a place close by to leave the car; the District would limit parking close to the Court, he reasoned.

That evening he walked to Capitol Hill and circled behind the building to its east, or back, side, across from the Court, the same route the congressmen would take from the Capitol. Ultimately, it was the layout of the Court building that interested him. He wanted to memorize how it looked from different perspectives. The expanse between the buildings brought a smile to his face. He took special note of the barriers already in place—a forecast of where he'd find the demonstrators—and the platform, still under construction, from which various leaders, including the president, would speak.

THIRTY-NINE

The United States Supreme Court building was one of the most beautiful and majestic buildings in the world. Architect Cass Gilbert, who completed it in 1935, its first permanent home, had looked to ancient Greece and Rome for inspiration. He chose the Neoclassical style of a Greek temple to reflect democratic ideals. Its sculpture, inside and out, depicted mercy and symbols of justice. Could one imagine other imagery? Would political appointees be able to match that imagery?

Gilbert's material? All-American marble, the timeless stone of longevity and beauty. For the exterior walls he chose Vermont marble; for the inner courtyards sparkling, white Georgia marble; cream-colored Alabama marble he decided should dominate the interior walls and floors.

The main entrance of the Supreme Court looks to the west, facing the U.S. Capitol building. Gilbert chose marble for the Corinthian columns that supported the pediment. Along the molding just above the columns and at the base of the pediment are the engraved words, 'Equal Justice Under Law.'

Sculpture is central to the building's overall design. Symbolic statuary fills the pediment. The central focus is Liberty, guarded on either side by figures who represent Order and Authority. Although they are metaphorical, the sculptor, Robert Aitken, carved the figures in the likeness of real people.

At the far left Chief Justice William Howard Taft represents 'Research Present'; at the far right Chief Justice John Marshall embodies 'Research Past.' Second from the left is Senator Elihu Root, representing 'Council.' Architect Cass Gilbert is third on the left. Third from the right, also representing 'Council,' is Chief Justice Charles Evans Hughes, who talks to Robert Aitken, the sculptor of the pediment and second from the right.

Below all this, seated marble figures occupy either side of the steps to the main entrance. On the left is a female figure, the *Contemplation of Justice* by sculptor James Earle Fraser. When the sculptor gave 'justice' form, Western tradition (Greek and Roman) suggested the symbolic image be female.

On the right side of the entrance is a male figure, also by Fraser. Sometimes called the Guardian, the Authority of Law, or the Executor of Law. Like the female figure, the Guardian of Law holds a tablet with the inscription LEX, the Latin word for law. A sheathed sword is also evident, symbolizing the ultimate power of law enforcement.

On the back, or east side of the building, rarely seen by tourists, the words 'Justice the Guardian of Liberty' appeared on the molding above the columns.

Herman A. McNeil carved the sculptures above the columns and molding onto the eastern pediment. At the center are three great lawmakers from different civilizations — Moses, Confucius and Solon.

The Court Chamber was also represented by columns and marble: walls and friezes of ivory-vein marble from Alicante, Spain; floor borders of Italian and African marble; and two dozen columns of Siena marble from Liguria, Italy. Some said Gilbert's friendship with Benito Mussolini helped him obtain his marble.

That was then. But what of the future?

♠

FORTY

August 16. The anniversary of *Hendricks*. Dénouement.

The space between the Capitol and the Supreme Court had begun to fill with people by early morning; many had arrived before dawn; some slept in tents. Most were happy, as though the day was just another excuse to party; others seemed angry. The latter were the ones with the bullhorns and speakers.

One could also distinguish the protestors based on their music, the aroma of marijuana (or not) and, obviously, their signs—signs that would ease the work of Downey and Vanni:

'THERE ARE NO DANGEROUS WEAPONS
THERE ARE ONLY DANGEROUS MEN'

'FEAR HAS NO PLACE IN SCHOOLS'

'IT'S BETTER TO HAVE A GUN AND NOT NEED IT
THAN TO NEED A GUN AND NOT HAVE IT'

'MORE KIDS, FEWER GUNS'

'AN ARMED MAN IS A CITIZEN
AN UNARMED MAN IS A SLAVE'

'PROTECT CHILDREN NOT GUNS'

'GUNS HAVE ONLY TWO ENEMIES:
RUST AND LIBERALS'

'YOU CAN PUT A SILENCER ON A GUN BUT NOT
ON PEOPLE'

The Metro and Capitol police already had their hands full controlling the anger and potential violence, and it wasn't even 7 A.M!

♠

Three hours later, as his shift began, D.C. Metro police sergeant Tom Ferguson double-checked his equipment belt that held his weapon, radio, cuffs, and Taser before exchanging a final joke with the desk sergeant. He left City Hall and walked toward the 'Black and White' where his partner, Joyce Atkins, waited.

Tom had taken up the cause of law and order nine years earlier. He didn't have an ulterior motive—an agenda. He didn't have what some have called a 'cowboy' mentality, an expectation, perhaps, that many might have about an Irishman. Not interested in throwing his weight around. Not a gun enthusiast. He simply thought people should obey the law. 'If not,' he often said to his wife, Louise, 'you got anarchy, and everybody loses.'

Some in town thought the pairing of an Irishman and a black woman from Talladega, Alabama, unlikely, even wrongheaded. Her first experience had been with the university police at Tuscaloosa's Stillman College. But there it was. Neither of the principals at Metro thought it odd or wrong, but tongues never stopped wagging.

So, the Irishman and the Black woman went about their routine until early afternoon. Then, as warned, they'd need to be ready to respond to trouble at the Court. That trouble began to manifest itself shortly before 3 P.M.

♠

Clinton Downey approached the tree line on the north side of the Supreme Court. His immediate purpose was to scout the police line and barriers for the easiest place of entry. Considering the police presence a few yards ahead, his appearance was extraordinary—bold. It broadcast the trouble Ferguson and Atkins had been told to expect.

Dressed in camouflage and over that a harness of

ammunition clips (tactical gear), Downey carried what anyone familiar with shootings in the United States with high numbers of casualties would have recognized: a long rifle that appeared to be an assault weapon. A .45 caliber pistol hung from his waist.

Suddenly, he heard (felt) a shot. He recognized the whooshing sound of a silencer-equipped, high-powered rifle. Startled by the suddenness and his proximity to the sound, it confused him that he saw no one.

"Hey, a**hole!"

The voice raised the hair on the back of Downey's neck. His head jerked left and right. He spun around to his left, trying to detect the source of the abrupt voice.

"Up here, a**hole!"

Downey turned slowly to his right, crouched, and looked up. As he did so, he pulled the .45 from its holster and shifted into a firing position. The move was smooth and all of one piece, as though he had practiced and practiced.

"Get the f**k out of here, ass …"

The man in the tree never finished his sentence.

From his hip, Clinton Downey fired one shot at the voice in the tree. A scoped rifle fell to the ground at Downey's feet. He dodged and turned his back, fearing the weapon might go off.

FORTY-ONE

Tom Ferguson and Joyce Atkins were only blocks from City Hall after a day of routine but uneasy patrolling, when the car's radio crackled sharply.

"Shots fired! Shots fired! Supreme Court. All units respond! SWAT … You read? …"

"Step on it, Tom!" Joyce Atkins shouted. "I've got the Remington and the helmets."

Tom Ferguson pressed the accelerator to the floor, and they raced toward the Court. His adrenalin had kicked in.

"We're just about there," he said in a near whisper, as though he wished it weren't so. "You vested?"

His was a nervous question. Even a casual glace would have confirmed the obvious bulges and tight blouse.

Joyce gave him a curious look and nodded that she was wearing her protective vest.

The black and white screeched to a stop behind the east side of the Court. People were running in every direction.

"Dispatch! We're going up to the Court!"

"Roger, 502, SWAT and backup should arrive any second. Other Metro and Capitol Hill officers and Guardsmen are on the west side."

"You take the Remington, Joyce. I'm getting the automatic in the trunk. This guy's gonna have automatic weapons, and there may be multiple shooters."

"Police!" Joyce screamed at a crowd pouring out of the entrance. "Move!"

They did so with alacrity when they saw the heavily armed pair running toward them. Ferguson and Atkins had no time to sort through them for a possible shooter. They had to assume he, or she, was still in the building.

They circled cautiously around the building at a distance until they had the street, plaza, and steps before them. Only then did they become aware of the bodies that littered the street, the plaza, the presidential platform, and the steps leading up to the building. Neither officer could distinguish the dead and wounded from those who had dropped to protect themselves.

"Where's the shooter?" Tom shouted at a terrified female just fleeing across the street.

"I think in those trees," she gasped, pointing. "Hurry!"

The sound of shots continued. Tom recognized the sound of law enforcement small arms and the unmistakable boom of an AK-47 style rifle, of which he'd heard far too much in Vietnam. But what alarmed him most was his certainty that the killer had converted his Kalashnikov from semi- to fully-automatic.

The pair ran zig-zag across the street and plaza, then up the steps where they took cover behind two columns. They now had a clear view of the trees west of the main building, if not a specific target. Before them, people in frenzied panic and terror ran or ducked for cover; some used bodies for protection.

Men they took to be Secret Service crouched or stood behind other columns for cover and fired clip after clip at a target or targets in the tree line not yet apparent to Tom and Joyce.

"Stay together. We don't know how many there may be," Tom commanded. The firing, which to Tom sounded automatic, continued.

They raced to the end of the outdoor hall of columns on the northwest corner. Then, coming from the columns to her right at ninety degrees, Joyce came face to face with an armed man in a camouflage jumpsuit. His manner appeared to be that of someone on a casual stroll. He was also reaching into a satchel for something as he made the turn to his left and ran smack into Joyce Atkins. Was it another magazine? Busy with the satchel, he hadn't yet looked up.

"Drop the weapon! Police!" Joyce screamed as she slipped to her haunches next to a column, making herself small and somewhat protected.

Clinton Downey, taken by surprise, finally looked

up, and with one arm raised his Kalashnikov toward Atkins.

Before Atkins could react and Downey could drop the magazine and fire, Tom Ferguson pumped five shots into his torso from his semi-automatic Glock.

The impacts slammed Downey against the wall. His now useless rifle and the magazine fell clumsily from his hands and clattered to the marble floor at Joyce Atkins's feet. She raised up and kicked them aside, still pointing her service weapon at the downed man.

"I'm going after others, Joyce. Make sure he's KIA."

Downey, his body relaxed and akimbo, sat slouching against the blood-stained column, his right leg folded awkwardly at the knee under the left and his arms dangling down, palms up. His head lolled to one side, and a bloody, pinkish froth began to trickle from his mouth. His eyes rolled upward once as Atkins felt his neck for a pulse, then froze open. She saw he wasn't wearing a protective vest, which to her suggested a 'suicide by cop.'

Tom Ferguson encountered one or two men he identified as congressmen from their lapel pins. They had been hiding behind columns on west corner of the building.

"Is there another shooter?" he yelled at them.

Too frightened to speak, the lawmakers shook their heads from side to side or crossed their arms wildly in a manner indicating 'no.' Nevertheless, Ferguson continued to search throughout the building. By now, additional Secret Service agents, National Guard SWAT teams, and Metro SWAT teams had joined him in securing the White House and its grounds, along with Secret Service agents present at the time of the assault. Emergency vehicles of every description and jurisdiction, along with dozens of ambulances had descended on the Court.

♠

Bodies of the dead and wounded littered the plaza and steps. Rounds from Downey's converted Kalashnikov had rendered some of them unrecognizable. Shredded arms dangled loosely, held in place by tendons. Decapitations. Perhaps eight to ten lawmakers or staff ran into the open from behind rose bushes or columns. The subsequent investigation and forensic examination (recovered slugs) revealed that Downey was not solely responsible for the toll of dead and wounded; many victims were hit in the crossfire between Downey and lawmen.

Near the podium from which the president had been speaking and just feet from where Tom Ferguson stood minutes earlier, a man lay on top of a female covered with blood not her own. President Gloria Addison, still frightened out of her wits, finally spoke.

"Help me."

Ferguson recognized her, of course. He rolled the man to the side. He had taken multiple hits. The man's earpiece dangled from its spiral cord. Ferguson knew then that the man was Secret Service.

"It's Bob Skinner," the president said. "He must have been hit just as he threw me down. The first shot, which came from a tree over there, she continued, pointing to a line of trees and bushes on the north side of the Court, hit him in the shoulder, I think. He took more hits but was on top of me by then."

"Are you hurt, Ma'am?" Ferguson asked while he checked Skinner for a pulse.

"Is he …?"

"Yes, Ma'am. He's gone."

"Did you see what happened to the second shooter?"

"Second shooter? I didn't realize there was a second."

"Yeah, right after the round that hit Bob. The sounds were different."

Ferguson looked around the garden for medical personnel.

"Tom!" the president yelled as another Secret Service agent ran up to the toppled podium.

Ferguson thought she meant him, but it was Tom Lester she had called out to.

"Madam President, are you hurt?"

"No, no, but Bob Skinner is. He saved me.

Lester bent over his partner, and then looked up at Ferguson. Both men understood that Skinner was dead.

"I'll take it from here, officer," Lester instructed. "Thanks for your assistance."

Ferguson left the president and Lester, and, acting as a one-man triage, began to check the people on the ground for any sign of life.

♠

When investigators released a list of the casualties, the number of dead was a staggering ninety-seven with thirty-four more wounded, some of them critically. The toll was especially high because the victims were crowded together; individuals couldn't break free of the mass; bullets passed from one body to another. They were sitting ducks for Clinton Downey's machine gun. Fifty-three of the dead were male and forty-four female. The press insisted on a further breakdown, as so many of their numbers, nine, had perished. The number of Capitol Police, Metro Police and National Guardsmen was a tragic eleven dead.

The FBI spokesman ended his summary by reporting that thirteen congressional colleagues of Senators Westfield and Brook and nine journalists had died in Clinton Downey's minutes-long fusillade. The FBI's list included neither the senator from Wyoming nor the junior senator from South Dakota. When trying to account for the safety of all lawmakers, investigators learned that both had been at home, either in Georgetown or Chevy Chase.

FORTY-TWO

In the hours and days following the courtside slaughter, police interviewed surviving witnesses, including the wounded and those who had escaped unscathed.

Some claimed they saw the man eventually identified as Clinton Downey—they remembered his clothing in particular—emerge from the trees and bushes north of the building and immediately open fire. His bold, camouflage outfit had caught Metropolitan police officers, Capitol police officers, and National Guardsmen by surprise, despite the elaborate preparations made to ensure a peaceful protest. According to surviving officers, the lawmen first took the gun-toting man as one of their own.

Once Downey broke through police lines, having cut down nearly a dozen of them, he faced police reinforcements and unarmed citizens, members of Congress and police reinforcements. The civilians suffered heavy casualties as Downey stormed from one protected area to another, usually behind vehicles or marble columns, replacing magazines as rapidly as he was able while firing, hiding, and dodging the blistering fire of increasing numbers of lawmen. He did so until he reached one too many columns and ran into Joyce Atkins.

♠

The after-action investigation moved swiftly along multiple lines. One of those became more complicated (confusing) when forensic examination of a bullet fragment removed from Robert Skinner's body came neither from a police weapon or Downey's Kalashnikov.

The solution to the mystery bullet resolved within a day when National Guardsmen discovered a body dangling from a tree north of the Court building, held there by the man's foot caught in the fork of two branches. An M24 sniper rifle still lay at the foot of the tree, which stood in the same thicket from which Downey had emerged, said witnesses.

Fingerprint analysis confirmed the dangling man to be Paul Vanni and the mystery fragment from his M24. Those conducting the review of events, including an autopsy, found one of Downey's bullets nestled against Vanni's spinal cord after it had passed through his heart.

Investigators' best guess about how the man in the tree came to be dangling was that Downey, who had been hiding among the trees, saw or heard the man fire and assumed he was a law enforcement sniper. So, he took him out with one shot. The autopsy physician said that Vanni never knew what hit him. There had been no co-ordination between Downey and Vanni.

♠

Evidence gathering continued along another line. Of principal interest to those investigators was the phone found on Downey's body and, because the 'dangling man' had shot at the president and missed, hitting Robert Skinner instead, his phone as well.

Downey's phone contained nothing incriminating. But Paul Vanni's held incoming and outgoing numbers, even though Vanni, the dilletante hit man who apparently knew nothing about managing phone content, must have thought he had deleted them.

FBI and ATF forensic experts went to work at once on each number, time of the day, and cell tower pings. Their sophisticated equipment and help from mobile phone providers determined several suspicious calls had emanated from a specific location in the Hart Senate Office Building.

♠

FORTY-THREE

Investigators worked diligently and swiftly. Three days after the massacre, FBI and ATF agents arrested Senator Stephen Brook at his home without incident. Brook, who now found his life in far greater danger than when sitting on the back of a bucking Brahma bull, could withstand neither his wife's tears nor his interrogator's questioning 'techniques'; he had no answers when confronted with forensics that confirmed his calls to and from Paul Vanni.

In the presence of his lawyer, who recommended cooperation in a plea arrangement intended to spare his life, Brook gave agents the name of his co-conspirator.

Perhaps the senator should have stuck to bull riding; he was about to endure a far more severe fate.

The FBI determined the conspiracy went no further. It remained only to find and bring Senator Westfield to justice.

♠

Senator Hiram Westfield moved faster than Brook's confession and the FBI. He had always doubted Brook to some degree, which causes one to wonder why he recruited him to the plot in the first place. He had to have considered the possibility that Brook would give him up, which now caused him, finally (too late), to question why he'd brought the South Dakotan into the scheme in the first place. Still, Hiram Westfield proved as weak as his partner and a coward as well.

Having questioned a half-dozen witnesses to Westfield's behavior on the day of the massacre and the week after Brook gave him up, the FBI determined the senator had fled to one of the seventy-five countries with which the United States had no extradition treaty. Flight manifests out of Washington's Dulles International revealed that Westfield had chosen one of those countries near the bottom of the list: Vanuatu.

♠

A Melanesian archipelago in the South Pacific, Vanuatu consisted of 13 principal and several smaller islands about 500 miles west of Fiji and 1,100 miles east of Australia. The islands extended north-south for 400 miles.

Westfield's ticket, which cost $2,100 and change, took Westfield on an exhausting journey from Dulles via Alaska Airlines to Los Angeles International; Fiji Airways to Fiji's Nadi International; and on to Port Vila International on Vanuatu.

Westfield's bank records, which the FBI subpoenaed, showed he had purchased a small bungalow there two months before the massacre. Obviously, he intended to spend the rest of his days on the beach.

Gloria Addison was not one to allow something like a non-existent extradition treaty stop her from carrying out the justice Senator Hiram Westfield deserved. She signed a finding that dispatched a crack team of Navy Seals to Vanuatu. The Justice and State Departments be damned.

♠

Following that fateful afternoon at the Supreme Court, now steeped like so many other places in America—schools, churches, stores, theaters—in bottomless terror and sorrow. Americans armed themselves again with unrequited questions and directed their anger at politicians on both sides of the aisle.

Their questions were always the same: 'When will you do something to fix the Second Amendment?' That question always went unanswered. But now Congress itself had joined the sad ranks of those countless places bathed in the blood of people from ages five to eighty-five. Would this time be different? Surely. The victims were principally the lawmakers themselves.

Some had said Congress would only act to limit the Second Amendment when congressmen lay dead. Now, thirteen of them were among the scores of dead. Would the lawmakers act?

♠

FORTY-FOUR

Professional Congress-watchers didn't have to wait long for an answer. The lawmakers, unmoved by the carnage at the Supreme Court that day, did nothing to shape the Second Amendment to a society in which weapons of modern warfare, not 18th century muskets, outnumbered its roughly 300 million people. The NRA had reached deeply into what money in its bank account and investment portfolio held and waved them like a magic sword in front of those who wanted to believe in fairy tales.

So, the killing continued in all the usual killing fields, places where young men with assault weapons, who thought of them as they did the video games they played incessantly, knew they would never face opposition—schools, churches, grocery stores, musical concerts, darkened night clubs—wherever unsuspecting people gathered in large numbers.

♠

Supporters of the Second Amendment reiterated their standard alternatives to guns: mental illness and the need for even more guns. Yet, in the aftermath of the attempted assassination of the president and the massacre of the amendment's opponents—and supporters—no state increased its budget allocation for mental health.

Some states did, however, pass laws that required teachers to arm themselves. In one of those, a gunman, believing the teacher in his target classroom had followed the law, shot her as soon as he walked through the door. (After the round passed through her body it pierced the classroom wall. Searchers discovered what remained of the slug 350 yards beyond the building.) Then, the murderer slaughtered seventeen of the teacher's children before police could end the rampage. The teacher had not armed herself. Her mother told investigators she couldn't afford it and had received no support from the state that required her to do so.

Across the country people announced in unctuous and smarmy tones that they held the victims and their families in 'their thoughts and prayers.' But the killing continued, which prompted a wag in California to opine that God had long since tuned out the phonies, being too busy listening to the prayers of sincere mourners.

♠

The Navy Seals, overtrained for their assigned mission but not unhappy with their destination, traced Hiram Westfield to the White Grass Ocean Resort & Spa on Tanna Island at the southern end of the archipelago. They found him lounging in a beach chair at water's edge, sipping a cool Mai Tai—his last it turned out. According to the Seal commander's written report, Westfield cried like a baby when handcuffed and trussed up like a hog.

Criminals who try to overthrow governments do so in part because they believe those governments corrupt and incompetent. They make that assumption at their peril. Hiram Westfield was a case in point.

He had arrived in Vanuatu steps if not miles ahead of the law, he believed, on a cushy, first-class ticket. He went home hog tied and tossed unceremoniously onto the cold, steel belly of a cavernous C-130. In the beginning, he whined a lot, mostly about his being a senator, et cetera, a nuisance the Seals ended with a strip of duct tape. Unfortunately, Westfield had neglected to shell out a nickel to bring along his lawyer.

As the giant plane ground east toward the United States and Washington, D.C., Westfield lay on its floor for twenty hours in his own filth with an occasional sip of water provided grudgingly. The vibrating turbo engines prohibited any chance of sleep. The Seals had not taken kindly to someone believed to have been behind an attempted assassination of the president.

♠

At both senators' trials the juries gave short shrift to anything the defendants' attorneys said, a heartless, quick, and unsympathetic dismissal. They convicted Westfield and Brook of conspiracy to murder after deliberations that lasted two hours in Westfield's case and five in Brook's. Jurors who spoke to the press following the Brook verdict reported they had to overcome some sentiment among jurors to account for Westfield's manipulation of the younger man.

What form of justice would the court serve up? History offered a mixed legacy of possible outcomes:

The first recorded execution in Washington, D.C, a hanging, occurred in 1802.

The U.S. military hanged Mary Surratt in 1865 for conspiring to assassinate President Abraham Lincoln. One might suppose that Surratt's fate did not bode well for Hiram Westfield.

Throw in Charles Guiteau, executed in 1882 for assassinating President Garfield. Add Guiteau and the defendants' chances grew ever more grim.

Events years earlier should have buoyed the senators' hopes. The federal government had secured the death penalty for murders occurring in the D.C., but the Supreme Court nullified it. The District Council followed the Supreme Court's lead a few years later, and a referendum not long after that confirmed the Council's action against the death penalty, 2-1.

Nonetheless, the verdicts handed down by Brook's and Westfield's judges might still have caused the senators to wish for speedy executions. Both were remanded to the warden of the United States Penitentiary, Florence

Administrative Maximum Facility (USP Florence ADMAX) to serve 'life sentences without the possibility of parole.'

"What does that mean?" Brook asked his attorney, who blanched at the thought of answering his client.

"Senator, I regret to say it means you will die in prison. While you live, they'll confine you twenty-three hours a day. Guards will take you out for exercise and a phone call, if earned, for one hour each day in handcuffs and shackles at any time of the day or night. They'll restrict your diet to ensure you can't use your food to harm yourself or to create unhygienic conditions in your cell. You might get one with a shower, *if* they feel you earned it."

"What else do you know you aren't telling me?" he demanded.

"Do you really want to know?"

Hiram Westfield sat a few feet away.

"Tell him!" Westfield shouted. "Tell the little weasel!"

The attorney glared at Westfield, then looked back at Brook, pausing to consider the wisdom of continuing.

"Senator, the facility is best known for housing inmates deemed too dangerous, too high-profile, or too great a security risk for even maximum-security prisons. These men, and there are over 300 of them, include spies and foreign and domestic terrorists. Not even Charles Mansion qualified, and Timothy McVeigh asked to be executed rather than continue his confinement in such a place.

"Are you telling me these men and others might be a danger to me?"

"I'm afraid so, senator. Among other things."

Brook buried his head in his hands and began to weep.

"Get him out of my sight!" Westfield screamed.

Now, Brook wailed.

"For God's sake, man, pull yourself together. Don't give them the satisfaction. There's always the McVeigh alternative."

Both senators survived less than five years at Florence ADX. They began the remainder of their life sentences at medium security prisons in different parts of the country.

♠

Cheryl Brook and Miriam Westfield divorced their husbands, reverted to their unmarried names, and began to carve out new lives in different states. It was as though they had entered 'witness protection.'

As the two children of the former Ms. Brook, now Cheryl Wilson, grew old enough to understand their father's crime, they refused abandon him. James (Jim) Brook visited his father once monthly, travel restrictions (distance) permitting, and Mary Brook wrote him regularly.

Miriam Westfield, now named xxxxx, with no children, remarried two years after her former husband's conviction.

FORTY-FIVE

Randolph Cavendish resigned from the Supreme Court six years into his lifetime tenure. One could easily characterize his short term behind the bench as both unenjoyable and undistinguished. He considered himself a legal scholar and purist, but it appeared he had no stomach for the politics.

Then, there was the courtside massacre. Whether he felt any responsibility for that remained a topic of conversation, opinion columns, and television interviews of the chattering class for as long as Cavendish and the Second, unamended, lived. He offered no comment or interviews and returned to his former life out of sight and sound of the world.

Cavendish's contribution to American jurisprudence at the highest level amounted to a brief, slavish devotion to the legacy of Mateo Ricci. He authored not a single majority opinion. The former judge from Rhode Island turned out to be anything but independent-minded.

And what of the Court? The apocalyptic event on the anniversary of *Hendricks* altered the pristine appearance of the Supreme Court building, which forever mocked the pretense of what transpired inside. Neither liberty, authority, order, the guardian or the executor — all rendered meaningless that August day—could protect the citizens of the United States and its lawmakers from the mayhem of their own creation. The stone-cold, unseeing eyes of the statuary solons were just that … stone cold and unseeing … incapable of forgiveness.

♠

President Addison ran for a second term. She chose to focus her campaign on gun safety, and much of the televised debates with her opponent concentrated on the Second Amendment. She lost a close race.

Before departing the White House for the last time, Gloria Addison left two items on the *Resolute* desk for her successor, the junior senator from Tennessee, Stuart Warren—a history of the desk and a cautionary letter, suggesting, among other things, the virtue of humility:

From the Desk of

Gloria Addison

Columbus, Indiana

January 15

Dear President Warren:

I'm taking advantage of the traditional 'letter to your successor' that by now you have now discovered on your desk, and I hope read, to congratulate you again on your victory and to leave you with some thoughts about one issue you will be facing among many others. I'm sure you know by now the issue I have in mind.

Your new job will fill your days, months and years with serious problems, not ones that until now were purely theoretical or resolved elsewhere. The transition from candidate to president requires adjustments, most of which you will find uncomfortable and inconvenient. That's a good thing. Don't fight it.

In our televised debates we discussed the Second Amendment and its interpretation by the Supreme Court. Those discussions occurred at my insistence due to their seriousness to the country and, frankly, your fixture to the position of an unqualified right of individuals to gun ownership. We argued and the American people spoke. But the election did not and will not stop the killing of innocents.

I believe you will not be surprised at what I have to say here. I think you would be disappointed were I not to speak again of what I believe to be an existential threat to the United States. There can be nothing more pressing for any president.

I want to speak of 'conformity,' which has become an all-too-familiar ritual regarding the Second Amendment. My starting point is the Court's originalists.

What can ... What *should* concerned citizens say of the legacies of the Supreme Court's so-called originalists? A crystal ball isn't necessary to predict the future pattern for which they took no responsibility: increased gun sales, particularly assault weapons; and an exponential increase in the frequency and lethality of attacks.

Will the pattern of mass murder cause Americans to conform to those events? To normalize them?

Will we conform to the ritual of 'thoughts and prayers' without knowing how the shallowness and hollowness of those words sound to the victims' families?

Will we conform to the media's ghoulish fixation on body counts, the victims, and to interviews with victims' families in the hope of showing audiences a tear or two?

Will we conform permanently to the habit of releasing the names of mass murderers, thereby giving them the attention they craved and an invitation to others (copy-cats) also desirous of a place in history.

Will we conform to the rituals of 'hardening' soft targets (read schools), putting children through lockdown drills, equipping them with bulletproof backpacks, and filling their precious childhoods with fear?

Will we conform to the millions of dollars in free media coverage the killers received, which instilled in future killers the desire to, as one of them put it, 'break a world record'?

Will the 'elephant in the room' refuse to budge and prevent us from budging it? Will Americans grow so comfortable with its presence they will see no reason to question Mateo Ricci's 'originalist' interpretation, which I would describe as a conclusion in search of a rationale?

Will we conform to a view of the Second Amendment that the men who wrote, 'a well-regulated Militia, being necessary to the security of a free State ...' did not mean to connect those phrases? Specifically, to 'keep and bear arms'?

We have the originalists' simplistic answer: 'No. The Second Amendment consists of two independent clauses, they insisted. The Founders were poor grammarians who didn't know what they were writing. Thus, those endowed with better writing skills must correct the error. And so goes alleged originalism ...

Since the originalists began with one conclusion, 'shall not be infringed,' logic required them to ignore or dismiss another, one that clearly did qualify infringement on the individual right to 'keep and bear arms.' In other words, they had to ignore the 'elephant in the room,' in this case the room being the chamber where decisions like *Hendricks* are handed down to the country at large.

How much longer will ... How much longer *can* the United States tolerate—live with—such egotistical logic in service, not to the country but to gun manufacturers and their lobby?

Last year, August 16 showed that a few congressmen were dispensable when faced with the business end of an assault rifle. Perhaps most astonishing, their colleagues cared nothing for their sacrifice. How many more children, including your children, President Warren, must die to line the pockets of weapons makers and their shills?

Remember, too, that the carnage of August 16 began with the attempted assassination of the President of the United States. That's not a threat, Mr. President. It's the times we live in.

So, the answers to my questions now rest with you. I pray you will find the wisdom and the courage to address them to the benefit of the American people.

Sincerely,

Gloria Addison

American Citizen

♠

Within weeks of Warren's inauguration someone leaked Addison's letter to the press, which treated it as a bombshell and the harbinger of an Addison comeback. It wasn't clear what President Warren thought of the former president's words, but speculation in the country about Addison's future in politics continued to lead news cycles for a time.

Many in Columbus, Indiana, and Washington, D.C., doubted former President Addison could put politics behind her. Had she washed her hands of it? Did she believe her loss made her a martyr in the cause of gun safety (control)? Did the ego that moved her to hope the letter she left for President Warren would somehow move him to show through action that she had misjudged him, misjudged the power of the gun lobby, or both?

♠

FORTY-SIX

Five years had passed since the voters spoke. Gloria and Sean shared a home but had not married. Formalizing their relationship, they believed, would add nothing to their love for each other or provide a sense of permanence.

Those who scoffed at the idea that Gloria would abandon politics after her presidency were correct in one sense. What those critics couldn't have imagined, however, was her unique, post-presidency political role.

She and Sean became speakers and grass-roots organizers for a national association calling itself, 'Communities for Gun Safety.' Its aim was to bring the voices of everyday Americans into the fight for common sense gun laws, to mobilize citizens who stood for the broadest cross section of 'community': mayors, city councils, parents, teachers, students, and survivors of gun violence.

The society lobbied for gun safety legislation at every level: local, state, and federal. It pushed hard for a potpourri of goals against intimidating odds: increased penalties for gun trafficking; education on responsible gun ownership and storage; closure of legislative loopholes that allowed gun sales without background checks; and support services to survivors of gun violence.

Long before the press tired of the former president's activities and moved on to subjects of greater remunerative advantage, as always is its wont, the bosses of the fifth estate had disappeared Gloria Addison to what editors and publishers consider oblivion, the graveyard of the back pages.

Meanwhile, Gloria and Sean were doggedly criss-crossing the country, making speech after speech, giving television interviews in markets large and small, writing opinion pieces for local newspapers, and employing their administrative skills in helping communities learn how to tackle the problem of guns before it was too late.

♠

The former president nonetheless wanted to think of other, more pleasant issues at breakfast that Sunday morning.

"Gloria?"

'Oh, oh, here it comes,' she thought.

The New York Times, not Gloria Addison, had commanded Sean's attention for several minutes. As she preferred that nothing distract from her breakfast, she found his inattention and then his interruption annoying. She stopped eating and gave him a look that said she wasn't interested. He noticed but persisted anyway.

"Brookings did an interesting comparison between your term and Warren's on gun deaths. Some interesting stats."

"Oh, Sean, please. I'm so tired. I've worked so hard. So hard. It's making an old lady of me. Do I have to think about this on Sunday?"

"I don't agree about your aging, but I think this analysis might give you some satisfaction about your four years.

"Really? Satisfaction? The voters sent me packing."

"Well, during the third year of your administration there were thirteen states in which gun deaths outpaced automobile deaths. In your last year it was fourteen states."

"I can't get excited about that. Why should we celebrate being ahead of car crashes?"

"I know, but there's a bit of a rainbow above those numbers."

"Huh?"

"I think you should hear this."

Gloria took another sip of coffee and leaned back in her chair.

"Okay, Honey, if you must."

"In the four years of President Warren's term, the number of those states I mentioned previously rose steadily and alarmingly above automobile deaths, from twenty-two states—up from fourteen in one year—to thirty-five in another!"

She stared blankly, trying to take in what he'd just told her. Finally, she spoke.

"So much for the message I left Warren. I honestly hoped it might move him in another direction. Some rainbow, Sean."

"There's one final sign of his not taking your advice ... if you can stand to hear it. I think you should. We might find a use for it when we go back on the road."

"You're going to insist, aren't you."

"Not if you'd rather I didn't."

She stared blankly, neither at him nor anything else he could discern. He knew the look. It meant she wanted him to continue ... and she didn't. He chose to ignore it.

"Okay, then. I promise this will end your torture. Ready?"

"Yes, yes! For God's sake, Sean, get on with it!"

"The numbers and influence of those who acknowledge the dependence of the bearing arms clause on the need for 'a Well-regulated Militia' ... Well, that elephant went the other direction, it diminished, as the originalists insisted it should."

"All this was to cheer me up, Sean? You do have a perverted sense of good news."

I didn't say it was good news, only that it confirms the points you made to Warren."

Well, leave it to *The Times* to provide us with depressing news about colossal egos and the pretense of omniscience. It makes me even more tired than I felt earlier ...

"If the country ever turns away from the likes of Ricci and Cavendish and their originalist mentors, and starts thinking about the lost lives and futures of innocent children … Then, I won't feel tired any longer, and *The Times* with its 'good news' will be welcome at my breakfast table!"

♠

DEBTS

My principal debt with this book, as with all my fiction, is owed to Sheila Ross. It pleases me to say that, although the expression alone does not account for the sum of my gratitude. As she has for my other books, Sheila read and re-read the manuscript (I'm a frustrating writer for the copy editor; I constantly edit and re-edit) for consistent character behavior, context, grammar and spelling.

Wikipedia supplied information on subjects beyond my familiarity: *hypertrophic cardiomyopathy*, the *Resolute* desk, Franklin expedition, Roger Williams, Sons of Liberty, militias, the 'silent generation,' Camp David, treason, Secret Service, Starfish Prime, the Medium Rare restaurant,

Supreme Court building, USP Florence ADMAX (ADX Florence) and so forth.

Ed Asner and Ed. Weinberger, *The Grouchy Historian: An Old-Time Lefty Defends Our Constitution Against Right-Wing Hypocrites and Nutjobs*. New York: Simon & Schuster, 2017, offered thoughtful Second Amendment points that supplemented my thinking.

♠

AUTHOR

Stephen Carey Fox comes from a Midwestern background. He attended DePauw University and the University of Cincinnati and served in the Navy as a Heavy Attack bombardier/navigator. His teaching career at Humboldt State University spanned four decades.

Steve is the author of award-winning articles and book-length oral/documentary histories of the relocation and internment of Europeans of enemy nationality in the United States during World War II.

He turned to writing fiction for the pleasure of 'telling lies for fun.' His books consider crime, history, feminism, reminiscence, family and contemporary political, economic and social issues.

Steve writes from behind northern California's 'Redwood Curtain' in Willow Creek, a village renowned as the home of Sasquatch (a.k.a. Bigfoot) and 'medicinal' gardens.

Made in the USA
Columbia, SC
11 August 2024

39827353R00169